Murphy's World

Ian Murphy

Murphy's World

All Rights Reserved © 2003 Ian Murphy

Published by Inkblot Books

Dayton Ohio

www.inkblotbooks.com

ISBN 1-932461-05-1

Printed in the United States of America

Murphy's World

Essays From *Martial Artists Wired*

Forward

In the early 90's, there was a group of dedicated martial artists who discovered each other online; it was new territory at the time, without the vast greatness of the Internet as we now know it. They belonged to the now-defunct Prodigy Online Services, created a small corner of the message boards for themselves in the Hobbies area, and created a bond of fellowship through their mutual interest in the arts.

Then, following the lead of other online services, Prodigy decided to step away from the flat rate service they had been offering, and they began to charge by the hour to access to their service.

So many people decided to leave Prodigy, yet wanted to stay in touch, that a snail mail newsletter, *Martial Artists Wired*, was created. Over time it evolved from a 10-13 page thread holding friends together to a major online e-zine, with contributors from all over the world.

In 1996, the founder and editor of *Martial Artists Wired* asked me to scratch out a monthly column; my thoughts and musings on anything martial arts I wanted to write about—especially if I could figure out a way to relate the martial arts to Corn Flakes. I was honored to be asked, and continued the column until late 1999.

Since I stepped away from the column, people here and there have managed to find me online, and have asked for copies of old columns. So this is for them, the six people who regularly read my column, and the two who became fans.

Table Of Contents

If You Give A Dance, You Gotta Pay the Band

"...Life, is better left to chance. I could have missed the pain, but I'd have had to miss the dance." Garth Brooks, from his song, The Dance.

I had listened to that particular Garth Brooks song many times, never quite hearing all the words, until a friend sent me an audio tape containing nothing but that song. Her goal was to assuage some incredibly hurt feelings over an unexpected and unwanted divorce, after having listened to my repeated whining and moaning and groaning, and after hearing my once-spoken wish that I had never, after all, married in the first place.

Her purpose, I gathered after truly listening to this song, was to remind me that I could have spared myself the pain of a failed relationship, avoided the pain of the ensuing loneliness, but the what end? Surely somewhere in all those 10 years there were some good times. At some point the woman's name had brought a smile to my face instead of a grimace, and at some point her name tumbling from my lips was accompanied by a light in my eyes.

It was never all bad, not even in those last days when I discovered to my horror that although I was happily married, my wife was not. The pain was nearly blinding, and the thoughts that crossed my mind were inevitably preceded with "if only," but there was good to be found among the rubble, if I knew where to look.

Had I never met the woman, never dated her, had I never married her, those final days of heartache and agony would have never been, yet I would have missed those times when she did bring the light to my eyes, the euphoria at hearing the words, "Yes, I'll marry you," I never would have known the simple delights of the small things she did as a matter of fact on a daily basis.

I would have danced alone.

Not too long before I was made aware of her growing dissatisfaction, and the fact (not the probability, but the fact) that she was divorcing me, I found in my martial arts training a certain amount of pain and discomfort. It was surprising, too, as I approached my classes with more enjoyment than anything else, and was anticipating a tremendous amount of success. I was a star pupil, and had been asked to test for the honored position of Assistant Instructor without being a black belt and having just a little more than 3 years of training in my martial arts resume. My confidence was such that I assumed the test was a formality, and began the hunt for the rank belt that would distinguish me from other red belted students at my dojang, purchased the required uniform, and began to think in terms of approaching other students with ways to better enhance their training time.

The test itself was nothing out of the ordinary: ritualistic performance of poomse by an entire group, oral quizzing on individual students on subjects ranging from dojang protocol to how to care for ones' uniform, point sparring and free sparring, and defense situations. Then came the final test of the day, something I had done only two or three times before: board breaking. The breaking technique was my choice, but the board had to be broken on the first try, and broken cleanly. I opted for the technique I knew would be foolproof for me, a flying sidekick.

This test, I remember thinking as I set myself for the four or five steps I needed to take, was much too easy. Obviously a given, one designed to guarantee my success. As I took the steps, jumped and chambered for the kick, I grinned in spite of myself, because I knew I was going to be the next Assistant Instructor, passed ahead of some other more advanced ranked students. Then, is spite of the confidence dripping from every pore in my body, my foot sailed over the board. I managed to pull back just enough to avoid killing the student holding the board, but not enough to avoid breaking his nose.

That was it. I had failed the test, I had let myself down, and there was nothing left to do but walk away and hope that I would be given another chance soon. Never mind the man on the floor writhing in pain. I had failed. Me. I was humiliated. Not once in my cloud of disappointment did it occur to me that I had very nearly killed my partner, and that the damage to his face and his psyche could be irreparable. I wasn't going to be awarded my rank.

I walked away from the dojang and did not return for several weeks, preferring to wallow in my own misery, and the realization that I was (in terms cited by a friend) a very large anal aperture. More concerned with my own misfortune, I allowed myself to ignore a fellow student and a friend in pain of which I had been the cause. I was too embarrassed to return.

In the time I remained apart from the dojang I received on short and To-The-Point phone call from my instructor: I was indeed still welcome in his school, and could return. There would be a price, as he felt I was in dire need of an Attitude Adjustment. I would, not could, return the class the following day. I accepted the unspoken message that I was welcome if and only if I returned to class the next day.

It occurred to me that I could walk away entirely, resume training someplace else, or to forego any further formal instruction and simply train on my own, seeking advice and technical help from other connected friends. It also occurred to me that although I may have blundered through the various phases of adolescence, my actions spoke otherwise. An important authority figure in my life was opening a door for me, and I dared not close it without seeing what was on the other side.

With outside encouragement from a close friend, I returned the next day, and found myself in an odd position of being a student yet not being part of the school. My training consisted of relegation to a small corner of the training floor, located near the bathroom, where I performed, usually in deep horse stance, basic punching and blocking. On rare and welcome occasions Master Rodrigues would wander past me and gruffly order "Kicks," or the dreaded "Pushups." I spent more than one entire class performing nothing but pushups.

I spent nearly two months in my corner. During that time I was persona non grata, a nameless, faceless being occupying space and nothing more. The hope that I would be allowed to return to class was something rarely allowed myself. Admittedly, I would have given up if not for the warning of another student of TaeKwonDo: sometimes we will leave a student punching air for two or three months to see if they really want the training, or if they only want the belt. At some point, if I stuck with it, I would no longer be the Disgrace of the Dojang, and become a student again. With encouragement I decided to stick it out.

Two weeks into the New Year I was admitted back into class.

I could have lived without the humiliation. I could have done without that pain sandwiched around the grief of divorce. I could have easily gone on my merry way of trouble-free training, secure in the knowledge that as a star pupil I was guaranteed my place in the dojang. I could have easily lived without it all. Would I have grown without it? Who knows? I suspect, though, that surviving the humiliation of my own ego and subsequent idiocy will make me a better martial artist in the long run. I want the training, not the rank.

Those words will remain a part of me for a long, long time: I could have missed the pain, but I would have had to miss the dance.

How Much Training Time Is Too Much?

You spend every possible moment contemplating martial arts. You think it, you dream it, sometimes you even eat it. The day is not complete unless you have spent in excess of an hour training MA—longer if you have a class (or 2) that day. Your personal library is comprised 95% of martial arts related reading materials, and you subscribe to 4 or more MA magazines. All or most of your friends are in the martial arts. You work your job to pay for your training, or your job *is* training. You get home from class and your first impulse is to open an MA book or magazine, or to go online and find other martial artists with whom to discuss your training.

As nicely as possible: get a life.

Training in the martial arts does give one an edge. Dedicated MAists are usually in shape and barring injury are physically healthy. Training can give a person confidence and boost self esteem. It can also lead to a one-dimensionality in personal character.

Consider what you would do to achieve the rank of black belt—or 2nd or 3rd or 4th dan. Would you pursue that goal to the exclusion of non-MA related activities? Give up hobbies?

Risk relationships? Would you even recognize if you did any of the aforementioned?

What happens when your instructor requires your attendance the same day your spouse or child has a function they would like for you to attend? Who loses, the family member or the instructor—and are you afraid of the ramifications if you choose family over art? Who's opinions and feelings count more?

Think carefully. Most of us at one time or another have chosen art over family. The problem lies when that choice is made consistently. Some spouses are amazingly tolerant of what it takes to become a proficient martial artist, yet even the most understanding spouse will eventually reaching the breaking point. If your spouse or significant other has ever said to you the time spent training has become too much, do you back off the training some or do you become defensive and deny it?

Children in the martial arts are an entirely separate problem when it comes to dedication bordering on obsession. The "dedication" may or may not be their own; the existence of the little league parent within Martial Arts is not a new phenomenon. Yet, without the opportunity to explore other areas of interest, a young MAist can become embittered toward training, or become a stagnant individual. There are other sports, other interests that need to be fostered in a child— even if that interest is vegetating in front of the TV for a short time. How can a child know what his or her interests are if not encourages to explore the vast range of possibilities? Kids need time to PLAY—without adult instruction or interference.

Adults in martial arts have more personal control over their training lives, and all-encompassing training is their choice, presuming the adult is emotionally healthy and not falling prey to instructor pressure. the question would be WHY an otherwise normal healthy adult would dedicate an inordinate amount of time to training. On average an adult can benefit as much from 3 classes a weeks as they can 6 or 7 classes a week. Anything more is overkill. Those days off give the body and the mind a chance to recoup. Off days are ideal for cross-training—something that can be shared with non-MAist family members and friends. Run together, bike together, swim together, just do it together.

If you're missing out on your kids' personal triumphs because you wanted "just a little more time" training, or your spouse has begun to wonder out loud that you may be spending too much time training, listen. Martial Arts has a valuable place in life, but it is not life itself, and there are so many other valuable things to try.

Obsession in the martial arts in not something to be proud of, it's something to be afraid of. Take a chance to see what else fits into your life. Become a whole person, not a one dimensional character.

Fill Up An Empty Form: The Value Of Poomse

I read a quote once; I don't know who said it, and I have to paraphrase, but it made me think. *Forms are like barrels; they're empty until you put something into them.* That's easy enough to dismiss as more martial arts claptrap, and I did just that, until it kept running through my mind while trying to figure out what to do with a female member of my staff.

From 5am-7am Monday through Friday my staff assembles for what is ostensibly referred to as "defense tactics." The primary purpose of this endeavor is to teach and prepare them for real life defense situations. I do not, for certain reasons, train my staff to flee from defense situations, something I otherwise strongly advocate. What is required is clean, precise and decisive intervention in an otherwise out of control situation. In other words, while I prefer the people on my staff to remain safe and out of harms' way, I expect each and every one of them to emerge from any physical encounter victorious and unscathed.

Which brings me to this particular female staff member, who in nearly all respects is the ideal employee. She is knowledgeable and attentive to detail, physically fit and otherwise fully capable of performing her duties. The single flaw—and a major one—is that the idea of hitting and being hit would freeze the woman with fear.

My dilemma: what to do with a respected staff member who cannot be transferred to another department and a less strenuous position, and who is psychologically unable to perform a major function of her position. Fire her? And waste all the other expertise she has to offer, no longer have access to her vast intellectual resources and varied base of knowledge?

Dismissing her was not a notion I found palatable or acceptable.

What then? How could I get past the walls of fear? I had tried everything I could think of from cajoling to outright threats: *hit me and hit me hard, or you're out of here.*

She offered to quit.

Unacceptable.

In a less stressed situation, or in a typical martial arts training situation, I would take a student from the very basics and take the time to build upon those. When someone is placed on my staff, under my supervision, their initial training is already completed, having been overseen by someone else. I have no control over those basic skills.

In most cases the basic skills are strong enough that they slide right into defense training with few problems. This woman—Trish (not her real name)—demonstrated no confidence in the basic skills that I *know* she possessed.

That quote continued to tumble around in my head. If it's empty, fill it.

Seems simple enough.

Fear is an emptiness; just replace it with something else, like confidence.

When I began my own martial arts training I already considered myself somewhat proficient in defense. Uncle Sam saw to that. I approached training as a means to expand my experiences in defense. What I discovered was a joy in training; poomse training in particular had a allure for me. Forms brought to my attention an angle to fighting I had barely before considered. It was more than strengthening of ambidexterity and timing, more than the honing of technique.

Visualization

Fear is prompted by the unknown. Deep down I was beginning to question that what appeared obvious on the surface—that Trish was afraid of being hit—was the true root problem. She knew in certain terms how to fight, how to react. She witnessed enough to understand that most physical contact and all physical contact conducted during staff training is not fatal. Our training track record is excellent; aside from a few bruises and wounded egos, no one has ever drawn blood or broken a bone.

It occurred to me that the real fear was the unknown—not knowing what comes next, not being able to see past the immediate technique.

With this uppermost in my mind I offered Trish a final chance—take a paid suspension from field work and begin individual training with me, or find alternate employment.

We began very basically; front kick, roundhouse kick, sidekick. The first day I introduced her to her first martial arts form; very slowly, very basic and uncomplicated. I added an unexpected twist: for each technique within the form I asked her to tell me to what she was responding. What is that "other person" doing?

To a student of the martial arts, this is not a new concept. Most take it for granted that there is an unseen opposing response in our forms. To someone with previous training in a nonstandard combative martial art, the notion is a revelation.

Forms offer an opportunity to engage those basic techniques without the threat of contact and harm. Beyond the obvious and accepted benefits of forms training, the confidence they instill and the range of training they encompass can be invaluable. Forms offer the ability to see beyond the kick or the punch—they offer visualization, and are a stepping stone to more advanced technique, and to contact.

With proficiency in basic technique and forms, we progressed to light contact in full protective gear. With the confidence of being able to perform those forms well and sustain light contact without harm, we progressed to more difficult forms and technique. As she developed confidence in her ability to pick apart a given form, to analyze its composition, she slowly began to find the courage to withstand more strenuous contact.

Did it work?

After several months of one on one training Trish rejoined the rest of the staff for regular defense training. In doing so, she also taught me one can have *too* much confidence. On demand to hit me—and I expected a punch to the chest—the woman caught me in the side of the face with a well placed crescent kick (and yes, I hit back). I learned not to take her for granted, and she learned contact is not always fatal.

Without the confidence building aspects of forms, I believe I would have lost a valuable member of my staff. The option if using forms as a training tool even in this "non-martial arts" venue is one I will freely exercise again if need be.

If it's empty, I'll put something it in.

Empowering Women

Women in martial arts are no longer a rarity. Walking into a martial arts school and encountering a large female student population is no longer as surprising as it was 20-30 years ago. Still, there are far fewer females than males entering the martial arts, and fewer still adult females willing to embrace the vigors of training.

Why?

In recent years the trend in psychology has been to examine unconscious motivations for behavior: why people do the things they do. Most of those explanations are too neat, feeble excuses that pass as reasoning to give credence to otherwise inexplicable actions. Drug use, bullying, promiscuity, and a host of other societal ills are brushed away by the wave of the psychological hand: your mother abandoned you, your father abused you, your friends teased you as a child, well of course you're afraid to trust and to love and to venture beyond your own doorstep.

Those explanations are too convenient. They lend a large and validating hand to people who have genuinely suffered in one form or another to adapting into and adopting the mold of a victim. They are not valid reasons for a person to mire themselves in continuing series of disappointment, trauma, and bad decisions. They are, at best, excuses.

I am not trying to be unkind, or refusing to understand the maladies of life that place stress on an individual psyche, or belittling true suffering. I am sympathetic to pain and dis-advantage. I do, however, believe that life is a series of choices, and any single individual has the power to make those choices that will help bring himself above the circumstances that would otherwise label him as a "victim." This doesn't place blame at the feet of the victim; it simply acknowledges that anyone, regardless of circumstance, has the choice to rise above it all and move on.

I have a very close female friend; in most respects she has the right to lay claim to the title of victim. She would otherwise be able to rightly claim that life dealt her a dirty hand, and she would be able to justify turning inward to her-self, to shy away from society and men in particular, to have become a promiscuous young adult and self abuser. The first time I met her over 23 years ago she sported a large, red, hand-shaped welt across her face. Over the next couple of years I witnessed numerable bruises, broken bones, cuts re-quiring stitches, none of which she never offered explana-tion, and at such a young age no one ever thought to ask. In hindsight I now know the cause; at 12 I could never have fathomed.

In mid-adolescence she encountered male brutality in the guise of a 19 year old male acquaintance who, after sev-eral beers, determined that the very act of accepting a date meant "yes," and no matter what, she would not return home as innocent as she had left.

As a young adult, a new mother, she witnessed the attempted abduction of her 2 month old infant; it was unsuccessful largely due to her own quick reaction time, but the stamp of trauma was burned into her psyche. Anyone who has ever loved a child can understand the enormity of the act.

Under the accepted actions of today's notions of victimization, she could easily have embraced the accumulated baggage of her life and turned it into a series of bad choices, disappointments, and reckless behavior. Yet, she has not. Unpredictably, her emotional outlook is keen and optimistic; she harbors little fear other than a few odd personality quirks. Why has this person, to whom life has been determinably unjust, not fallen prey to the role of victim?

"Whatever I do, I am responsible for...the things that have happened changed how I view the world, and changed me...ultimately, whatever I do in spite of anything is my own responsibility." What she chose to do ultimately, was rise above and beyond the bad things in life to create the good.

A large part of that was the decision to never again allow herself to be in the position of physical abuse. "I've been there," she once told me, "I'll never be there again...and I have little patience with women who wrap themselves up in rape and use it as an excuse to keep the world out. All men didn't do it. One man did. That's all anyone needs to remember. But I'll still work to protect myself."

This all brings me back to my original question of *why* more adult women don't seek practical, long term instruction in self defense. While the numbers of women in martial arts grows, so does the population of women with no training in the art of defending themselves. Women have made tremendous strides in all areas of life, a reckoning force in business, finance, management, government; they raise our children— some single handedly—run our homes and our lives and keep track of the infinite minute details that enable us all to live better. Women are increasingly present in facets of life that as little as 25 years ago were considered male-only domains.

Yet, still, in a male-dominated arena where women *should* be present in vast numbers, they are not. The demand of equality is being met with a stubborn resistance to empower.

It's a sad fact; women are often brutalized at the hands of men. Women can prevent this, protect themselves against it, yet in large numbers do not.

Is it because society in general frowns upon women engaging in combative activities? I need to ask why should women *care* what society (meaning men for the most part) thinks about the act of female survival. Women traditionally rise past the male-societal view of acceptable female activities; why is self-protection different?

In my own little world of ideals, our children would learn basic defense as a matter of course through our schools; our daughters would be armed early on with the knowledge and skills to protect themselves from the untoward of life. In Murphy's World women would comprise at least half of the martial arts community, making the choice to embrace self acceptance and defense of oneself over an ill-formed societal view. Women would buck the norm, shuck away the accepted notions of the acceptability of victimization.

If you empower a woman, she will never be a victim.

Birth Of A Dojang

I was present at my son's birth 14½ months ago. He came into this world at a whopping 9lbs 8oz and measured out to 23 inches long. A big kid. Big even for his 5'10" mother to carry for nine months and then bare. After being on the sidelines throughout that entire pregnancy, coaching through the labor, and then observing his birth, I've come to a major conclusion.

That was a piece of cake compared to trying to open a dojang with friends.

A good epidural took care of the pains of childbirth (women, don't yell at me, I'm only presenting the facts as I was told.) There is no available anesthesia for 3 friends trying to find space, students, and equipment for a TKD school.

Unless beer counts...

The first notion of Tweedledee, Tweedledum, and Tweedledumber opening a school together began 2 years ago when one of them (don't ask who is who, we seem to take turns being the latter, depending on the opinions of the women in our lives...) tested for and was awarded his first degree black belt. Greg (TK) Scott, after years of juggling a hectic personal schedule and creating time to train where it just didn't exist, had attained his first major goal in the martial arts: becoming proficient enough to earn his black belt. I had the honor of sitting on his testing board, and when the time came for him to be awarded his belt, our instructor passed the belt to me and allowed me to tie it around the waist of the man who had been my closest friend for over 10 years.

Master Rodrigues commented in a rather off-hand manner that he expected to see the two of us teaching together someday, and God help the MA community when we finally did. The idea was appealing, but be both agreed it would never happen. Not through lack of desire—it was a simple matter of circumstance. TK had his job, which required more time than any human ought to give of himself, and my job was taking me halfway across the country. Just two weeks later my very pregnant wife and I jumped into the Mustang ("your babe-mobile" she disgustingly calls it) and left. In all honesty, I never expected to see TK face to face again.

Still, I was not all that surprised just a short time later to receive e-mail from him. The gist: "I'm at my parents' house in Illinois, I quit my job, I am UNEMPLOYED. How the heck do I find another job?" Easy…you come to work for me.

Over a year later, and a lot of personal growth and experiences behind us—I have a son and am expecting another child, he found *the* woman and married her before she could get away—Master Rodrigues' foresight is close to fruition. TK realized working for me is not his ideal (and who can blame him?) What he loved to do, though, and was discovering a natural talent for, was instructing in the martial arts.

Who, though, he wondered, would sign up at a school where the instructor was only a 1st degree black belt, regardless of how good? Perhaps if his 3rd degree buddy would coinstruct and help teach advanced students? Perhaps...better yet, what about that confirmed bachelor with the studio apartment, one barely living green plant, and a fire-engine red Jag convertible? Dack Hunter, 5th dan, no way would he be interested into cutting into his social calendar to take part in a new dojang. Would he?

The conception had taken place nearly 2 years before...the first labor pangs began over a pool table and beer and sodas. While we all stood numbly watching my wife run the table (do not *ever* challenge this woman for cash in pool or bowling unless you want to leave broke...) the subject was tentatively raised.

Dack looked pensive for a moment and then wondered aloud "What's in it for me?"

A share of any profits...the satisfaction of teaching...passing along your skill and knowledge to children and young adults...the tradition of promoting growth in the arts.

He shook his head no.

"I was hoping for cookies. Fresh, hot, right out of the oven chocolate chip cookies and *not* baked by either of you two YoYos."

The bargaining had begun in earnest.

I looked at my wife and smiled. "You bake *great* cookies," I said hopefully. [it should be noted that TK's wife, although a wonderful woman, is forbidden by federal law to step into a kitchen with the intent to cook] My beautiful, charming, talented wife sank the 9-ball and took me for another $5 and asked, "Well what do *I* get out of it?"

It should be noted here, too, that what men considered really good payment for services rendered, and what women consider good payment are worlds apart. I scrubbed 5 bathrooms till they shined, Dack got his cookies, and we were on our way.

The decision to open a dojang is an easy one. It's the details that can drive you nuts. Do we want to be "commercial" or not? Small school, medium, large, or grand-honking-huge? Just a dojang or a fitness center of sorts? Even if martial arts only, do we want fitness equipment, space for individual workout, and someplace for kids to play? Lease or buy? Build or make use of existing real estate? Why the HECK isn't there just a Dojangs R Us store where we can go and pick out what appeals to us the most and charge it to VISA???

"Space," Dack proclaimed, "I hate those little places where there's no room to really thrash around. And a pool. We need a pool."

"Weights and a playroom," I vocalize, wanting toys for myself as well as space for my kids.

"Cheap," Tk wants, thinking in terms of his wallet.

What we did agree on is that these kinds of decisions are best made over 3 large pizzas and a couple of pitchers of beer. It also raises the question of alcohol consumption among school owners…for three men who actively dislike beer, we were drinking an awful lot of it.

As with most important decisions in our lives, the cool-headed, reasonable, and intelligent answers came from the women who run our lives. "Lease…weight room…viewing room where the parents can see their kids train, with toys and a TV for little brothers and sisters," was my wife's view. "If it takes off you can build your dream dojang later," was TK's wife's opinion. "I want my own office," was Dack's view. One long cold stare from the women convinced Dack that he could survive if he shared one office with the rest of us.

There was the inevitable rolling of feminine eyes with the warning, "Don't forget about bathrooms and dressing rooms."

Sure, like we would forget THAT…

"I have to clean bathrooms?" TK realized. "I have to clean stuff?" Dack and I both smiled and nodded. We have real jobs. This dojang is mostly TK's baby.

When your martial arts friends discover you are about to undertake the task of opening your own school, they *all* have opinions and want to be heard. Go with hardwood floors…no, carpet…no, tile… Use contracts…don't use contracts…buy mats, heavy bags, foam shields, lots and lots and lots of pine… Don't use white uniforms! If you build a pool, I'll teach for free…

The truth is, none of us need to make a living at this. Not even TK, who is now unemployed and spends his days searching high and low for the optimum place to begin our dojang (the benefits of a well employed wife.) We have the luxury of time and knowing that we won't have to charge an arm and a leg to students who train with us. We are, however three very different people with our own personal preferences and views on what we want and what we'd like to accomplish. TK just wants to teach; Dack wants a place to train as well. I just want a killer dojang and to be the envy of every instructor that has ever lived. Is that too much to ask??

The labor contractions are very close together; the expected due date of the birth of our dojang is around the middle of January. In a sense, I suppose this fulfills everyone's belief that we all are, in fact, real mothers…

Taking A Back Seat To Real Life

I realized something this morning, when, after much cajoling and reminding I sat down to plunk out my thoughts on martial arts and cornflakes (contrary to popular opinion, I'm not sure I *can* put a MA twist to breakfast cereal...) I haven't worked out—not in MA training—in nearly a month.

As a matter of course I work out every morning, 5 days a week, from 5am to 7am along with 25 other bleary-eyed, sleepy confused souls. We go routinely through warm ups, and then make a concentrated effort to beat the snot out of each other without leaving any welts, bruises, or drawing blood. And we're all very good at it, not a broken bone yet and little more than wounded egos. My morning workout is completed alongside the best of the best. It feels like I lose a good 5-7 pounds of sweat every morning.

It is not, however, the martial arts training that I love. We do no forms, we practice no combinations per se...we just train to hurt and not be hurt. Normally after work I get together with a few fellow MAists and really train—the concentrated training I need in order to feel good physically.

Real Life has a nasty way of intruding on the things you like to do. I like to work out; I enjoy sparring and forms training. It's as much a part of me as anything else. Or so I thought.

My wife is 6½ months pregnant. This has not been nor will it become an easy pregnancy. We have spent the last 6 weeks alternately holding our breaths in hopes that the tide will turn and not wash us away, to breathing in rapid, heady breaths when things look bright and we feel that everything is right with our world and nothing could possibly go wrong.

In early January, by the time most who read MAW see this, my wife will have undergone surgery to correct most problems, and God willing the bulk of what worries us most will be gone. And I'm not telling this to garner sympathy, or to tug at anyone's heart strings. It's just a simple fact of our lives. Our Real Lives. The part of life that in all honest truth, I would not want to go on without.

Then comes the realization this morning that something I thought was a tremendous part of my real life is in truth no more than a sidebar. Something informative and necessary at times, but it is not the bulk of my existence. I can live without it.

This isn't to say that I want to live without it. In the past I have been of the opinion regarding those who wish to take an extended break from training or who wish to leave it potentially for good, that it will always be there for them to return to. I don't anticipate my absence from training to be a long one at all, and in the meantime the plans for our dojang go on. TK has found a suitable location and renovations will begin shortly.

And yes, they will begin without me.

Is there a point to my ramblings? I'm not sure. I would like to think this realization—that I can abandon without thought my normal course of training—is of itself a lesson in martial arts. The truth is, as important as training is to most of us, it is not our everything. My world isn't a majority compostion of sweat and forms and the sound of a dobak snapping on a kick. Right now my world—the two most important components—is sitting on the bed with a copy of Dr. Seuss, trying to understand the complexities of the Cat In The Hat, and to understand that no, Trubble our House Cat cannot walk and talk and wear odd head gear. Tonight my Real Life will be lived in a very small corner of the world, huddled in front of a fireplace with the two people who mean more to me that the very breath that teases my nose and lips.

That other part of my life will be there in March when my daughter arrives. For now, I'm enjoying the best of it.

Elitism In the Martial Arts

It's like a sucking plague in the martial arts community, reminiscent of the old Ken-L Ration commercial for dog food: "my dog's better than your dog, my dog's better than yours…" Just substitute "art" for "dog" and you have the whole ball of wax in one neat package.

Everyone seems to think their art is "the best." Everyone thinks their information is the most correct, their instructor is the most knowledgeable, their art has the best foundation, and everyone else out there is to be merely tolerated.

I ain't buying it.

In the midst of a debate regarding the impracticalities of TaeKwonDo versus another popular martial art, I was reminded gently by a friend "Most are products of their instructors influence, and are blindsided by what they have been told." I find a truth in this; we accept on blind faith that when our Sabumnim or sensei tells us THIS IS TRUE, that is it true. He wouldn't lie to us, after all.

Perhaps not intentionally…but our instructors are also the product of *their* instructors, ad infinitum. The problem with this is that facts, when passed from one person to the next tend to distort until they no longer resemble the original truth. You can try this for yourself at large party. Gather everyone in a large circle. One person writes on a piece of paper a tidbit (usually in the form of gossip as this is better party fare.) He whispers it into the ear of the next person, who in turn relates the information on. By the time you get to the last person, that little slice of gossip—say, Thumper got drunk and let Murf get a tiny rose tattooed on her hip—can become a whole other animal: Thumper got wasted, slept with Murf and 5 other men, and now has a Harley tattooed on her ass. A very small tidbit of original truth may still be there…surrounded by a lot of clutter.

The changing of history and fact is human nature; we either don't pay close enough attention, or small pieces of fact escape us, and eventually one thing evolves into another. George Washington and the cherry tree is a myth, yet it was propagated for years to grade school children as fact because it was "good for them." George may have been a good man, and the story may have inspired a few kids to tell the truth, but does that make the distortion all right? It propagated the truth by telling a lie, plain and simple. It begun with a small tale told *as fiction* and became reality for hundred and thousands of American children and their teachers.

So what happens when an instructor tells his student "we do this because it's the way it has always been done, passed on through generations," when in truth he just didn't know? That student then passes it along to his students…and the fundamental truths change. With each varying art comes a varying truth. Which is the National Martial Art of Korea? Two arts I know of lay claim to this distinction. Do their students know any better? Probably not. There comes with that claim a certain amount of pride; with it a certain amount of snobbery and a tendency to look down at that "other art" making the same claim.

We're in America. Most of us are American, or natural-ized. Does it *matter* what the art is in another country? Per-haps noteworthy in passing curiosity, but does that fact change the content of the art, make it any more or any less effective? Change its validity?

I don't think so.

It comes down to some basic notions: all martial arts are more alike than they are different. To lay claim to having the best is at best a sales technique, used to drawn in and keep students. When asked for comparison by prospective students, how many karate instructors claim, "you don't want TKD, it's all sport." Or a TKD instructor may claim, "Tai Chi is a waste of time, it's just old people exercising in the park." Why not the truth? Why not simply tell the students "we emphasize differing points of fighting technique," and admit that most of the basic foundations are very much the same? Why bolster your art into something it has no right to claim to be?

If your art flourishes, it will do so on its own merit and the teaching strength of the instructors. There is no need to fill the students' heads with age-old propaganda and a big-oted view of other martial arts. There is no best martial art. Elitism has no decent place within martial arts. Teach, don't preach.

Would You Like A Little Cheese With That Whine?

Every MA school has one. Usually more than one. It's the student who always finds something to whine about, like clockwork, every single class. My stomach hurts…I pulled a muscle…I can't *do* this. Unfortunately by the time that student passes through the doors for the first time, whining is a habit not easily unlearned. It's a tool that has served the whiner well: Mom and Dad cave into it, for no other reason than to shut the offender up; *it works*. Most kids try whining, but with most kids it takes only once or twice of a parent explaining "I can't understand what you're saying when you whine," to stop the behavior. It ends about age 3 or 4.

But there's always one. And it seems in the martial arts, there's always 5 or 10. Those kids who have made it out of diapers and into preschool with whining as a firmly established, well oiled tool to get what they want when they want it, or to get out of anything they don't want to do. Martial arts and whining are like oil and water—they just don't mix well.

Whiners are annoying. They disrupt the class, they require extra attention just to get them to complete required exercises, oftentimes they are loud and unruly and a royal pain in the ass. No one wants to be around a professional whiner. Certainly no one wants to be in the same class with one. And who would want to be responsible for teaching His Royal Whininess?

For one, I would.

I'm not immune to the nerve-grating effects of a whiner. I am just as easily irritated as the next person. My own son is 18 months old a recently made his first foray into whining. It began innocently enough with a tummy ache and probably a headache, he felt lousy and he wanted attention right then and there, and in his toddler eyes he certainly *deserved* getting that attention—and a cookie—right on the spot. *MommyMeWantACookieOK?MeWantACookie!* *Mewannacookiewannacookiewannacookiewannacookie...MOMMMMMMY!* Knowing her oldest child wasn't feeling well to begin with, was out of sorts because a new baby had taken up residence in *his* old room, and life was just outright hard for little Alex, it would have been very easy for Mommy to kiss his little forehead and give him the cookie.

One of the things that attracted me to the woman in the first place was her intelligence. Alex did not get the cookie. He did get a kiss on his little forehead, and a hug, and was then told to go play in his room until he could ask nicely, and calmly. He did just that—he headed straight for his room, began to play with his cars, and promptly forgot there was such a thing as a cookie in this world. But the whining did not work. I have no doubt that he will continue to make forays into the world of whining as he gets older, and his success rate in getting what he wants will be the same: Mom won't budge. Neither will dad. Had she given in and handed over a cookie—something easy to do—the seeds would have been planted. Whining would have worked.

There's more to our stubborn resistance to whining than the fact that it's outright annoying. More than the notion that if our children are allowed to fall into that trap they will be disliked and possibly friendless as they enter school. Whining is an open invitation for trouble. Whining signals to the untoward that herein lies a victim. Whiners are often easy marks, more dependent on others to do simple things they could do for themselves, less willing to take responsibility for things they find unpleasant—it's easier to whine and complain long enough and loud enough until someone else gives in. When one lacks the skills of independence, however, one becomes open for someone more cunning, cruel, and untoward to take advantage of. It can range from being victimized by a school bully, verbal or physical abuse from school aged peers, or even harassed and abused by trusted adults.

This is the major reason I choose to train chronic whiners. I'm not a masochist; I don't particularly enjoy facing a room full of whiners, but I understand that on some level, my patience and unwillingness to yield to the nonstop shrillness of this habit may make a difference somewhere down the road.

The easy way out is get ignore the whining and push through the class, concentrating on the more attentive and perceptive students. The student who continually complains "I can't do this" will quiet down when told fine, don't do it. The "I-have-a-stomach-ache" students become miraculously cured when told to sit out and rest. "I pulled a muscle" is amazingly relaxed and refreshed and all smiles when given an ice pack and told to heal for a few days before returning. Those are easy, quick fixes to an ongoing problem. But those aren't the solution.

With most whiners a simple direct "do it" approach

works, as long as there is no malice, eye contact is made, and individuated attention is perceived on the part of the student. This doesn't mean stopping everything you're doing and concentrate solely on that one person; it can be as simple as verbally acknowledging the student's concern and stating firmly "I know you can do it." Then drop it and continue on. Often the student goes ahead and does what he was originally told to do. If not, schedule time aside from class to speak individually with the student. It is important to not belittle or tease; it is imperative to get the point across without anger that when in class you expect adherence to the curriculum being taught, and that you honestly know this person is not only capable of doing the required exercises, but that they can do them well, as well as or even better than others. A whiner has a fundamental need to be acknowledged and wanted; oftentimes that in itself is enough to spur them into working on eradicating the unwanted behavior.

When possible, parental involvement is the best aid an instructor can have in stopping the whining during class. A parent can become so immune to a child's method of communicating that the whining no longer seems irritating and is an acceptable form of communication. Most parents know their kids are whiners, though, and often feel powerless to stop it. While you can't control what goes on in the home, you can control what goes on in your school, and it is important to make the parents aware that while you will not tolerate any whining, you will always welcome that student into your school, and you would appreciate positive reinforcement at home of non-whining behavior.

With any child positive reinforcement generally garners favorable results. Sustained eye contact and firm control works with most people (in my own case, eye contact and simple direct commands enabled me to train past Adult Attention Deficit Disorder), as long as that is metered with genuine kindness.

Annoying as they may be, whiners should not be discouraged from continued training. Continued MA training can go a long way in addressing the self esteem problems that result from chronic whining, and motivate a child into self-correcting the behavior. And in the end, when it matters most, it may save them, not only from the hardships endured in the school halls, but from the realities of life itself.

When The Heart Matters Most

I debated writing this. The subject matter seemed self indulgent, self pitying, and designed to garner sympathy from people. It is private, and by nature I am an intensely private person. Private to the point I drive most people crazy avoiding simple questions as "what do you do for a living?" or "where do you live?" I don't like to talk about myself, generally. I enjoy my literary musings, thinking out loud and on paper, but to divulge information about myself or expose my personal life is uncomfortable for me. I prefer to keep private things private. Call it paranoia.

Most of my students know little about me, either. If they ask, I gladly tell them about my MA background, how long I've trained and with whom; I'll show them my rank certificates and even discuss what I liked and disliked about my own training experiences. I have pictures of my children hanging in the dojang office, and I'll gladly tell anyone who will listen about all the wonderful and cute things they do. Rachel's first real smile. Alex sticking toothpaste up his nose. A very young big brother sitting on Mom and Dad's bed, pretending to read Dr. Seuss to his baby sister from a Fingerhut catalog. But, I still tend to remain closed off when the inevitable questions surface. I just don't like to talk about *me*. Until now.

Last month, just short of turning 36 years old, I had a heart attack.

Why this seems important enough to write about still escapes me. I just know that I have to do it, and have been encouraged to do so by the people who love me, and the person who relies on me every month to tap something publishable out on the computer. Perhaps it is cathartic. And perhaps someone reading this might benefit from my own misery. Perhaps someone will take a good look at their life, and make some changes before they find them self lying on a gurney in the ER listening to a doctor muse out loud how a person in such good physical condition could have a heart attack so young.

Like many who have been involved in martial arts for a number of years, training with dedication and always looking for ways to perfect technique, I *am* in good physical condition. At 6'3" I weigh at my heaviest 195 pounds. My body fat is very low. I eat right—thanks mostly to a wife who zealously guards over my fat intake and will literally slap a ding dong out of my hand if she catches me with one—and my cholesterol hovers at about 130. There is no family history of cardiac disease in my family, other than some very, very old relatives whose hearts simply gave out in their 90s. I exercise daily, training in TKD, lifting weights, jogging; my life is very physical, and I benefit from consistent aerobic activity.

So how could I suffer a heart attack? Even a mild one? I do all the right things.

How?

Stress.

Like most other MA instructors, my primary job is not

teaching my art. I don't teach full time, as much as I would like to. My days last anywhere from 12-15 hours, after which I either teach, or run, and then go home to my family, where I am usually occupied with paperwork and family obligations. After the kids are in bed I generally unwind in front of the computer for an hour or two. I get perhaps 5 or 6 hours sleep a night. And I usually work weekends, teaching a class or two and putting in at least 10 hours at the office. And, the job itself is highly stressful.

With the combined lack of sleep for years on end, increasing workload, personal conflicts with friends, my year thus far was topped off with the death of my mother in late March. My carefully constructed walls caved in, and with a mixture of grief and anxiety, my heart sent me the strongest message it could: *back off and rest, or die.*

It was a "small heart attack;" meaning, for the most part, that it was a loud warning shot, and I was allowed to return to work after just 2 weeks. I took a month off instead. I did return to the dojang, not to teach or train, but to watch. And I watched very carefully. One of my partners in the dojang works out of the same office I do, has nearly the same amount of daily stress. His risk was as high as mine. With family history, perhaps higher.

And the students... Mostly young, fresh, and full of vigor, none seemed likely for the ER any time soon. But how can we know? I certainly never thought it would be me. The last thing I ever would want to see is one of my students laid up in the hospital for any reason, much less because of their heart.

Then I wondered, just how much responsibility do I have towards these kids, and the adults who train under me? Does teaching them self defense include the degree of self awareness that goes with understanding, fundamentally, how much the human body can take, and how to know when it's telling you to ease up? The kids who train daily, either by their own choice or their parents insistence, are they affected by the training process negatively? Is the rigorous schedule too much? Am I obligated to step in and say enough is enough, you're over training, so back off? Do I even have the *right* to express that kind of concern and interfere in someone's personal life?

The truth is, I don't know.

I refuse to be an instructor who purports to know all and pass out medical tidbits as fact when in truth they may be bits and pieces of a whole part. I refuse to pass judgment on the way a person lives, or how hard they train, even if to the exclusion of other facets of life. I may have my opinions, but generally unless asked I'll keep my mouth shut. But…in doing so am I an accessory to later health problems? Do I bear some responsibility if later one of my students keels over after class, as I did?

I think so.

While fundamentally I may have no right to tell a student anything at all about the conduct of their private life—even when diet and work and personal habit are in question—I do have a certain responsibility to impart enough information to give them the ability to make choices. I can't tell them that in order to train with me they have to give up undesirable habits, such as smoking and drinking or drugs, but there is no reason I can't make available to them the information that expounds on these habits' complications. I can't tell a student his work schedule is grinding and can kill him, but I can make arrangements for periodic stress reduction seminars and make these available to my students. While I can't make these a requirement, I can make them damned attractive by swallowing the expense and begging the students to be there.

I want my students to be happy, and healthy.

I want them to know I care.

I want them to *live*.

The message to me was loud and clear: make some changes and make them now. Embrace the training and teaching, but not so fanatically that it adds stress that I just don't need. And make it fun; if I'm relaxed, the students are relaxed, and we all benefit from it—something that goes right to the heart of training.

Don't Lick The Salt off Your Students

Last week, while my wife and I prepared dinner together, our 4½ month old daughter slept peacefully in her swing, and our 21 month old son Alex sat quietly at the table with a pad of blank paper and the word's thickest red crayon in hand. He was being extremely cooperative, scribbling passively while Mom and Dad readied his favorite thing in the world—food.

Now, Mom and Dad should know better. A quiet toddler is usually up to no good, but since he was there at the table within earshot and where we could see him by just turning our heads, we assumed there was not much he could do. We'd know if he slid off his chair to go anywhere by the sound of his sneakers slapping the tile. That occasional crinkle was just the sound of him going for yet another sheet of unsoiled, unmarked paper.

I finally looked up from chopping vegetables (with a knife, no fancy hand chopping techniques allowed in the house); innocent little Alex Murphy sat there at the table with an open bag of potato chips. He was carefully, deliberately, licking the salt off each and every one, and placing them in a pile on the table.

When told sternly it was almost dinner time and he was ruining his appetite (never mind I never should have left a bag of chips on the table) Alex looked up and calmly pointed out, "Daddy, I din' eat dem." He then picked up the bag and swore "I was gon' put dem back."

I have no doubt that this wide-eyed little boy was being very sincere and honest, and doing exactly what he knew he had been told: it was close to dinner time and it was too late for an afternoon snack. He had no intention of eating those potato chips. And he had every intention of putting them back into the bag when had licked off every bit of salt he could find. While my wife stood behind the kitchen counter, hiding a smile behind her hand and trying not to snicker audibly, I stood there faced with a predicament: let it go, praise his honesty, or criticize his actions.

He's not even 2 years old. I let it go. If I were half as creative as my young son, I'd probably try the same thing; my wife won't let me have the potato chips because she's seriously into keeping me healthy, but if I'd thought of it first, I probably would have licked the chips clean too. And I too could honestly say "but I didn't eat dem!" Aside from not being half as cute out of my mouth, coming from an adult it's less than honest.

I thought of my son and his potato chips yesterday while watching a class of new students warming up, at least half of them very sure they were about to die, and the other half convinced they were paying good money to be not so subtly tortured. Out of 20 students, 5 or 6 were giving themselves generous leeway in counting off pushups and situps, at least 2 counts for every one pushup. My initial reaction was to go over and correct the matter—to make sure they didn't cheat. But these were fairly young kids, and my own son popped into mind.

He didn't think he was cheating by licking the chips. He was, in fact, very sure he was keeping right in line with the rules, and to his thinking, he had every right to do it that way. I let it go when I realized his sense of right; while I couldn't let these kids forever double count, I could determine why they were doing it they way they were.

I approached one boy and got down onto the floor next to him, doing pushups right along side. "How many have you done?" I asked. He gritted through the strain and moaned "Eighteen, sir," and then added, "but everyone else is on 9." He was counting every time he went up, and every time he went down.

"Do you know why?"

"Yes, sir, they don't count as fast!"

In his eyes, no one was wrong—he was just counting faster. He didn't understand that we don't count until we're all the way up; fundamentally, he was very honest. He intended to do all 30 pushups. And he didn't understand why he was getting through them so much faster than everyone else. Everyone *looked* like they were going about the same speed...

I could have embarrassed this boy; I could have embarrassed the whole class. All it would have taken would have been for me to stop the warmups and bark out corrective measures. Or I could have corrected the class instructor and pointed out to him some of the kids were "cheating." The problem would have been solved, right?

Perhaps for the moment. But how would those kids have felt, and how would the entire class have felt?

Probably a lot how my son would have felt if I had snatched the bag of chips from him and barked "You *know* you were told it was too late for a snack!" Absolutely miserable, picked on, and hurt. In the same light my son was not trying to cheat his way around the no-snack order, these kids were not trying to cheat themselves out of their warmups. In the most basic, fundamental way, they were doing their best to do what was asked of them.

The most kind thing that I could see was to spend a few minutes and get my butt down on the floor with each child having difficulties, and quietly explain that they were doing great, but I wanted to show them how I count pushups and situps. And added, that if they felt better counting their own way, that was fine, but to double the number they finished on. The only confusion over that method was a young boy who blurted out, "but that will mean I have to do about a hundred pushups!"

Math was never my strong suit, either.

Our students don't always intend to cheat themselves; even when it seems deliberate, and it appears on the surface that you're dealing with a basically lazy person trying to avoid the sweat that goes with the work, there just might be an honest toddler licking potato chips in front of you.

Remember, harsh words sting.

Wherefore Art Thou, Teacher?

Dominick Micceleti is 8 years old; he wants to become a black belt so he can, in his own words, "kick my big brother's butt."

Sharon Foster is 42 and entered training to alleviate the repetitive boredom of her weekly aerobics classes and to push past the invisible wall that stymies her physical progress.

Victor Young is 18 and admits he has no idea why he decided to train; it just seemed like a good idea, and so far he's still happy with the decision.

Drew Rustin is 10 and is "only here cause my dad makes me.

When a prospective student enters our dojang one of the first questions they are faced with on a written survey is **WHY DO YOU WISH TO TRAIN IN A MARTIAL ART?** The answers are as varied as the students themselves; most answers are pat, practiced statements that say what they think we want to hear, which is an answer unto itself.

I prefer the honest answers, the ones that occasionally surprise me. There are no "right" or "wrong" answers to the question; if a student answers in a way that leaves any of us perplexed, stymied, or even laughing, (*I'm here because I had to either do this or take ballet and since I'm a guy I thought I would look really bad in a tootoo and those toe shoes are killers on your pedicure...*) we don't exclude that person from training.

Truth is, it doesn't matter **WHY** someone begins to train. All that matters is that they do. The reason someone begins training and why they continue generally changes over time. It's no secret that I began formal training in TKD because I wanted a black belt. It was an ego thing. Uncle Sam made sure I could fight and defend myself and those around me, but I **really** wanted a black belt in *something.*

Once I was there and training, that belt seemed much less important than it had before. I kept training for a variety of reasons, but primarily because I appreciated my own instructor's philosophy:

EVERYONE HAS THE RIGHT TO LEARN TO DEFEND THEMSELVES

It's a simple concept. Just teach someone what they need to know to protect themselves and perhaps loved ones. Give them the skills to avoid being a victim. Teach through caring and concern; leave intimidation at the door.

That simple idea became increasingly important to me as I encounter more and more instructors who don't seem to want to take the time to teach. They want students—but they want to hand pick each and every person who trains under them. They want "worthy" students. People worthy of the knowledge they have to impart. People who will perform up to par.

What a pile of egotistical, self centered, self important crap.

Instructors seeking "qualified" students aren't looking

for individuals to carry on their art; they aren't looking for ways to better someone else's life; they surely are not searching for someone to teach. They want training partners.

There is not one student in our dojang more important than another. The most talented student has no higher status than the student struggling the most to make the smallest progress. Each and every one of them has a fundamental right and expectation: to be taught to the absolute best of our abilities with no preconceived notions about what our students *should* be able to do versus what they can do, and no unreasonable demands on their personal lives and physical capabilities. The day we start hand picking students because they are more attractive to teach or because they are already physically capable of keeping up with us is the day we can no longer honestly call ourselves instructors.

If that person walking through your door just wants to learn to kick ass, or get in shape, doesn't have a clue, or just wants to earn a black belt, they still have that fundamental right to learn to defend themselves. Granted, you are under no obligation to teach them anything, but who needs instruction the most? Someone already skilled enough to take you on, or someone who isn't even sure why what he's thinking of doing is so important? What kind of instructor are you if you turn away those who need you the most?

Why a person enters into training doesn't matter in the least. What makes them stay, and work, and learn, does matter. People will change through their training—but only if they are given the chance in the first place.

In Defense Of Never Bowing

Several months ago our esteemed editor of *Martial Artists Wired* wrote a piece on Tradition (I Won't Bow...) Included in that piece were reasons to not bow to your instructor outside the dojang or dojo. As I recall, some of those reasons were a feeling of subservience when called upon to do so outside the training venue, and the adamant recognition that most of us reading MAW are of a Western Civilization, not Eastern, and are not bound to its customs. The rank thing ends at the dojang door.

I hadn't given it much thought since reading the piece. For the most part, I agreed with it. I find no useful purpose in bowing other than to show respect inside the dojang. The major difference is that I never have bowed to my own Instructor—and my students do not bow to me.

Is this aberrant? I don't know. In the grand scheme of things it doesn't seem to matter nor does it affect discipline in the dojang. My students do not bow, but they do call me "Sir," or "Mr. Murphy" while in class and are expected to extend that same courtesy to each and every student in the class. There are no first names during a class session. I call even the youngest student "sir" or "ma'am;" not only does it remind them that they are expected to use these terms, but it makes them understand that the respect is a two way street; I cannot expect my students to adhere to rules I myself will not.

So why don't I bow?

When I first entered training, the students *did* bow to the instructors. As I observed classes before signing my name on the dotted line, I watched them bow as the class began, bow every time they addressed each other personally, and bow at the end of class. It seemed to be a meaningless habit. Still, of all the dojos and dojangs I had visited, this seemed the most likely candidate for me to train in; the people were friendly and the students eager and willing and happy.

I scheduled a conference with the master instructor; I wanted to begin training with him, but I had one quirk: the bowing thing was not me, and I had to be upfront that I would probably never do it.

It didn't have anything to do with a feeling of subservience on my part. It had more to do with a day in 8th grade that sticks out vividly in my mind, and reminds me that we are not all the same and should never be expected to follow the same protocols.

I don't know what schools do nowadays, but I remember in elementary and junior high school beginning each day with the pledge of allegiance. We were expected to stand and place our hands over our hearts, and we were expected to mean it. It became one of those rote things you did at the beginning of homeroom, and never gave much thought to. I did it, and I was not even a U.S. citizen. Eighth grade opened my eyes: not everyone, even diehard U.S. Citizens, are willing to pledge allegiance to the flag, or to the United States.

That was the year of the Screaming Mrs. Pitman, an old

woman who probably should have no longer been teaching, but she was there, and she was bitterly adamant about all her slovenly, unkempt, no-good students getting off their butts and reciting the pledge. This year, though, there were two students who kept their young butts firmly in their seats, and refused to participate in the Pledge.

The shock, the horror…Mrs. Pitman turned various shades of red, and exploded. There would be no tolerating such ignorant, disrespectful, disgusting students in her homeroom. They either got up and did the damned Pledge, or she'd see to it they were not able to sit for a week (remember, this was nearly 25 years ago and in Texas, where spanking students was a daily ritual, known fondly as "getting your licks.")

It didn't matter: she could yell and beat then and threaten to have them beheaded during the next pep rally, but they were *not* going to get up and pledge allegiance. In the midst of ranting by a lunatic teacher, the brother explained that doing so would violate their religion. They pledged allegiance only unto God.

They left her homeroom; so did several other students, myself included when I related the tale to my father, who was so angry he turned more shades of red than did Mrs. Pitman. He marched to the school the next morning and physically removed me from her homeroom himself, and let her know exactly what this gentle Catholic man thought of her bigoted view of those with different beliefs.

The Screaming Mrs. Pitman episode popped into my head when I first saw people bowing to their instructors. I believe that no one, I explained to this prospective instructor, should ever be forced into displaying signs of allegiance they don't feel within themselves. And those same brave 8th graders, were they inside his dojang, would face the same scrutiny; they could not bow to him without compromising their religious beliefs. They could not bow to the Korean Flag. And truthfully, I felt very uncomfortable with the idea that what is essentially instruction in a fighting art would require adopting someone else's cultural ideals. I would certainly understand if because of this he did not want me as a student, but it was a point I felt strongly about, and felt obligated to state upfront.

It was never a problem for him; he in fact had an entire family who, for the same reasons, could not and did not participate in signs of loyalty pledges; they had explained up front that they could only bow down before God. He had wondered, in fact, if being unable to participate made them uncomfortable. And now he wondered if other students felt the same and were simply unwilling to say so.

I began training; I never bowed. The master instructor made it known that bowing was not obligatory, it was voluntary, and anyone who did indeed feel uncomfortable with the notion did not have to do so. Bowing to the Korean Flag ceased shortly thereafter when several parents expressed they had never liked the idea of their children bowing to the flag of a foreign country. They understood the original explanation of a dojang being somewhat akin to an embassy, and following the protocols of that embassy, but it didn't negate the fact that they did not want their children doing this, and in fact were fairly sure no Korean would walk into the U.S. Embassy and bow to the U.S. Flag.

I bring this whole matter up because I was recently approached by a parent whose child entered into training with us after several years under another instructor. He was concerned that we were not teaching the martial art as a whole, and that by not bowing we were missing something, not teaching proper respect.

There is something to be said for never bowing; not doing so detracts nothing from the art itself and does not have to be an impediment to discipline in the training hall. One partner in the dojang agreed to not have his students bowing, but he himself can't break the habit. And it does become a habit.

If it's a habit, there is no meaning.

So, no, students under my instruction will never be required to bow to me. All I ask of them is honest effort and courtesy, and an occasional bribe of freshly baked cookies.

When Commercial Isn't

I have a healthy disdain for belt factories; they cheat their students, take the money, and leave those who went to them in good faith in a precarious and potentially dangerous situation. All too often the skills they teach are basically worthless and sometimes taught by a disgruntled student of a reputable instructor who left somewhere after a year of training to open his own "school," names himself a high ranking black belt, and decries his new art to be the "real" thing.

I don't have a problem with commercial schools that aren't also belt factories. It would be nice to be able to teach full time and not have that other "real" job hanging over your head, to be able to give your students all the time they needed each and every day. I don't dispute what a commercial school may or may not charge; if someone needs to charge $80-100 a month per student to make a profit and live comfortably, and teaches good, clean skills well, I have no problem with that either.

I do have a problem, though, with the assumption that if a school *looks* commercial, it probably not only charges through the nose, but it is also a McDojo, or belt factory.

Take a tour through our dojang.

Upon entering you will be greeted in a reception area by either an instructor or older student; there is always someone at the desk. We don't require an appointment, and anyone is free to drop by and observe as many classes as they choose. If all you want is to watch classes as they are taught, you'll be shown the viewing room, which separates the main work-out floor via a two-way mirror; you can see the class, but the class cannot see you. You'll be told where the coffee machine is, pointed out the easiest way to the nearest restroom, and if you have very small children they can stay with you in the viewing room and watch TV, or watch the class, or read the comic books, or they can go across the hall to the play room, which is complete with crayon-friendly walls and supervised by a female student no younger than 14. You will also be told to feel free to ask any questions you may have, and to watch as many classes as you like.

If, instead of just observing classes you'd like a tour of the entire school, another student—or more likely an instructor—will take you through the facility. From the front desk you'll be shown the locker rooms, which are complete with showers, privacy stalls, and lockers. After that, you'll be shown the weight room (and reminded that if you are under 14, you will not be allowed to use this part of the school) which has several multi-station weight stacks, stationery bicycles, treadmills, and one free-weight bench (no one under 16 on the free weight bench.)

From there you'll be shown the playroom and viewing room, both equipped with large TVs, and the playroom—always supervised—has toys available for children ages 1-5. There are coloring tables, a LEGO table, and tons of building blocks. In the viewing room there are also plenty of books for younger readers.

Down the hall from the play and viewing rooms is a small library of martial arts related magazines and books, and a computer. You can lounge in one of the overstuffed chairs and read, or check out books at the front desk. If you are still in school and need a tutor, one of the other students will work with you here, and you'll have access to encyclopedias and online materials. If none of the students of the dojang can help, we'll find a tutor.

Across the hall is the entrance to the main workout floor. You won't be asked to bow upon entering, but you will be asked to remove your street shoes to preserve the hardwood floor. Along the longest walls are floor to near-ceiling mirrors. Stacked along another wall are the thick mats we drag out for teaching falls and throwing; in a padded cabinet (padded because *I* ran into when sparring once) are an assortment of weapons and sparring gear. The main floor is about the size of a gym floor, and an additional area about half that size off to one side used for those coming in early and wishing to work out alone, or stretch, or for private lessons.

After the general tour, you'll probably also be told that by February of next year our pool will be finished—not a huge one, but big enough for lap swimming, and shallow enough to conduct water resistance training. If you're interested, you'll be invited to attend our monthly nutrition classes, whether you become a student or not.

The school is bright, clean, it looks more like a health club than a dojang. I admit, it *looks* commercial.

We charge $25/month for the first student, $5 for each extra family member. If you can't afford that, we'll work something else out. If you can't pay period, we can work with that also. We don't use contracts. There are no testing fees, not even for black belt. Each student is given a *dobok* (*gi*) up front. We also lose money every month, but the building is paid for and we all have other jobs that pay our bills. We barter with other businesses to get some of the extras that we'd like: a local daycare center will soon be providing free drop off care for women attending women's only self defense classes, which we hope to begin in February. Some of our students receive free instruction in exchange for their expertise or help in the playroom and for tutoring; one of our students is a certified nutritionist and conducts classes on nutrition, another student has had years of experience as a personal trainer and helps teach other students to use the equipment in the weight room correctly.

We look commercial, but are we? And if we are, does it really matter? In the end, no matter how good the school looks and how attractive the amenities we are able to currently offer seem, the only thing that matters is what we teach, how well we teach it, and that it works. The day I believe we've gone off track and are compromising our art and no longer teaching viable self defense skills is the day I hang up my dobok and close the school.

The reverse can be said for the garage school. Maybe it doesn't have the aesthetic appearance of a large commercial school, but in the end if what you learn is better than what you would in the glitzy school down the street, you're much better off. If you have to sweat to get through it, to push yourself and learn to break through your limits, then it doesn't matter if you learn in my school, a garage, or the park.

We chose the amenities for purely selfish reasons. If we are commercial, I can live with that. If we ever just start selling belts, shoot me please. Just be sure to keep my body away from the pool—it's not paid for yet.

I Am Not Your Father

I have a wife and two kids. I adore the woman I married and I can't get enough of my son and my daughter; they are the first thing I think of when I wake up—I can't leave for work without giving each a kiss in their sleep—and they are the last thing I think of when I go to sleep. Concerns over them absorb my thoughts throughout most of the day. I love the sound of my childrens' laughter, I feel safe in my wife's arms. I deeply love them, and my life without them would seem less than complete.

I suspect any parent is the same; any man who loves his wife and any woman who loves her husband, or their significant others, has the same thoughts and motivations.

These people are our families. The ties that bind.

Generally I bite my tongue and let it slide when I hear others describe their martial arts schools as "real family." Other's perceived descriptions of the people they train with are generally none of my business. If it makes them feel better to adopt the notion that the people they sweat with are family, it's no skin off my nose.

It's generally just semantics. I seriously doubt they believe the dojo or dojang is one big honest to God family. It's just a term.

I'm even guilty of turning the phrase "family atmosphere" a few times myself. I use it more to emphasize the fact that our school is not of the old school; we believe in discipline for sure, but more over we believe in a caring attitude towards our students and actively encourage family participation. We don't adopt the militaristic methods of teaching; we use positive reinforcement and active verbal encouragement. Ideally, we would like the parents of our younger students training as well, if for no other reason that they understand what their children are really doing and what we are trying to teach them. Martial Arts for the Family. *Family atmosphere.*

However, in the most real sense, we are not a family.

I care deeply about my students; I understand that I am indeed a role model for them, and I highly believe in my partner's often touted *Lead By Example* proclamation. For this reason alone I choose to use as gentle a demeanor with them as I can and still instill good martial arts technique and discipline; I want them to have the stick-to-it attitude they will need to succeed not only in martial arts, but in all of life. The young sons of single mothers who train under me have, I hope, a good example of what a man really is. The daughters of exhausted parents do, I hope, see in me that a man can be tough and gentle at the same time, firm and caring.

But…I am not their father.

Would I be there for a student outside the dojang if needed and wanted? Of course. I don't think any instructor worth his stripes would not be there. I've attended a wedding so far, sweated out in the waiting room while a young student underwent serious surgery; I recently attended the funeral of the infant son of a student. Show me a first-lost-tooth and I'll be all smiles; tell me about that straight A report card you worked so hard to achieve, or confess that first crush that turns out to not be one-sided, and I'll be ecstatic. If a student is struggling in academics, I'll help find a tutor. I'll pay for it if need be. I appreciate not only being allowed to see parts of my students' private lives, I am honored when they choose to share it with me.

But, still, I am not their father.

I care; but my students are not my waking thoughts. My heart doesn't bleed for them when the bully in the nursery calls them a freak. I don't get frantic over bumps and bruises and skinned knees where they are concerned. I know that in a few years' time, they will be gone from my life—to date I have not been able to rid myself of even the most annoying blood relative. Hopefully the students will create among themselves a few life-long friendships, but I cannot allow myself to get so wrapped up in their personal lives that I lose the perspective necessary to remain objective about them. My heart does bleed for my own children; it aches for my wife.

A few years ago my fiancée—now my wife—wanted to enter training. She approached my instructor and asked permission to begin training with him. He was delighted; sure, of course she could. And because I had a lighter student load than his other assistant instructors, he assigned me to be her instructor. I was not only uncomfortable with the idea, I refused. This was a woman with whom I intended to build a life, not someone I wanted to push through the maze of forms and techniques and sweat. I did not want to be, in her eyes, her instructor on any level. The woman is my equal, and our relationship, I felt, should remain always on that equal plane. Any give and take that did put us on different footing needed to be because life simply designed it to happen that way, and never would I choose to be in a position of authority over her.

That equality cannot exist between and instructor and his or her students. In order for the instructor/student relationship to work there has to be some distance in order to maintain objectivity. I could never be objective about teaching my wife; I would either be too lenient or too harsh with her. I could never be objective about training my own children for the same reasons. We are too close; the love that flows between us and the bond that keeps us together won't allow for that kind of objectivity.

For that same reason, I cannot fathom the dojang members as being a family. Once that line is crossed and those feelings are allowed to surface, all objectivity goes out the window. I could not in good conscience sit on the testing panel of a family member. I could not be sure that I was passing or failing them on the basis of real talent and what they have learned and can or cannot do.

Where there exists a family atmosphere, there does not exist a family. And I believe that distinction is for the better, for the preservation, of our arts. That line in the sand might be blurry, but it's there, and for a reason.

Your First Responsibility

There are times when the training regime—through no planning—becomes not physical, but verbal. A strict, tightly planned class involving sweat and moaning and groaning might have been the agenda, but the students who show up, and the things they have on their minds, can change that before warm-ups are even halfway over.

Last week my intention was to conduct a conditioning class. No forms practice, no sparring—strictly conditioning, working them all until I could feel their stares at the back of my head like daggers of ice. I look forward to these classes; not because I particularly enjoy torturing people, but because I know that after it's all over, when they're standing in line at the water fountain, inevitably one student will grunt, "well that *did* feel good," and others will agree, even grudgingly. And I'm not a complete sadist. I participate as well as dictate.

This one day, in spite of my intentions, there was no sweat, no daggers directed at the back of my head, and no painful groaning. Eight male students, all in junior high, showed up for class and lined up promptly, ready to begin, all unusually quiet. Eight 12 and 13 year old boys just do not shuffle in quietly, and do not stand there without fidgeting at least initially, and don't murmur a sullen "Hello Mr. Murphy." Not unless their report cards have come in, or their very first term papers are due. Or both.

If one person, or two or four out of a class look listless, plans can generally proceed. When the entire class looks like they've already been beaten down and are only there for credit for showing up or to get out of cleaning their rooms, plans have to change. I did something I've never done before: had them all sit on the floor in a circle, and just talked.

It popped into my head to delve into Dan-Jeun breathing exercises, and to discuss self defense and the responsibility of using the tools of defense wisely. If I couldn't prod them into physically exploring their art, I could at least get them mentally and verbally exploring it. Pick their brains, see how much each knew not only about the things we had been teaching them, but to see if any of them had made attempts at learning about other martial arts. It could be an educational experience, enlightening and overflowing with wisdom. It could be a lecture...

I began by asking them what they knew of responsibility. I wanted to know where their hearts are, how they perceive the skills they have in accordance with the rules they have to live by. Do they understand that while I try to make most of the training fun, it's not a game and I frown on martial arts play outside the dojang? Do they grasp the fact that even in jest, a sidekick thrown to someone's head can have dire consequences?

While I am often stumped by the musings of my 2 year old son, I am rarely taken back by the things that pop out of the mouths of my adolescent students. It's not often that one single sentence uttered by a 13 year old can totally alter my train of thought, and derail me from what I intend to teach. And although I learn very subtle lessons from these kids everyday, it is rare that I find one thing floating around in my head for days after.

"Your first responsibility," said one student, "is to the truth."

No one laughed, no one rolled their eyes or groaned nor uttered the expect "God, that's so lame..." No one even looked at me as if needing an explanation. I was, in fact, no longer needed other than to listen, and perhaps because without the presence of an adult, the rest of the discussion might not have taken place.

I was given a glimpse of the world through their eyes. What I saw was a hypocritical glance at the things adults do and say to children, the very loud message of "do as I say and not as I do." We tell our children that honesty is imperative, but we don't teach it; we are at best poor examples. And they understand the mixed message better than we would suppose. They hear the words and see the opposite actions: have you ever lied to an police officer when stopped for speeding? Said your speedometer clearly showed you were doing the speed limit? Ever uttered the words "but the check is in the mail?" Do your criticize your government, when you didn't bother to vote? Ever share gossip with your spouse within ear shot of your children, even if you can't support the validity of what you're saying?

Our children *are* listening.

Even more, they are taking the things we say personally. I don't care for the way most of my students, especially my male students, dress. They come out of the locker room in jeans with legs wider that my shoulders, shirts 4 sizes too big, and pants slung down around their hips. Yet when one boy echoed how his father felt the same, he wondered out loud if his father ever bothered to look at his own high school pictures. "In the 70's," I was told, "you guys dressed like freaks."

I'm sure if I asked my father, he would agree.

When class was over, and these boys left, I realized that not only were their observations legitimate—adults tend to say one thing and do another, then criticize when our children follow in those footsteps—they were valid in everything. Not only in their private worlds, not only in how I apply my own logic to my own children, it applies in teaching them their defense skills, what I think of the art, any why I have drawn the conclusions that I have.

How many of us who teach are verbally critical of another art, even though we recognize that most foundations are pretty much the same, and that a student willing to learn and explore can get as much from another art as he can from the one you teach? How many students are blindly promoted through ranks regardless of skill to keep them and/or their parents happy? And how many students are outright lied to in an effort to gain their money for services, regardless of the quality?

At some point, through their own observations and study of the arts, the things we tell them will show true colors. If we tell them "this is the *only* thing that will work," they will know we are lying. If we promote above a student's real skills, we instill false confidence that can get them injured, or killed. If we take their money when we don't personally have the skills to teach, it's nothing more than outright robbery.

This young man was right: above all else, first and foremost, we owe them the truth.

What A Difference A Year Makes

It's late at night, and I am very tired. The house is eerily quiet, everyone else has long since gone to bed and fallen asleep. I tried to sleep, but tossed and turned, and unable to quiet all the thoughts tumbling through my head, gave up and quietly crept out of bed and turned the computer on. The day has been unbelievably long and physically wrenching, but not half so much as emotionally draining.

One year ago I sat quietly beside a bed, unable to sleep—unwilling to give in to night time fatigue—only able to fixate on the woman who was able to sleep, watching carefully the rise and fall of her chest, nearly counting every breath, muscles tensing at the slightest sigh or sniff, bracing against anything that might sound like pain or fear. The world could have collapsed around me and I wouldn't have cared; all that mattered that night, and in many nights preceding it, and for many nights to come, was that the woman live, bear a child in as little pain as possible, and recover. I wanted nothing more out of life other than her survival.

One year ago, though I'm not sure I would have admitted it to myself, the chances of her living through what turned out to be a horribly problematic pregnancy were slim at best.

Nature decided to make it difficult, a surgeon decided to give her a fighting chance, and the grace of God lifted her gently through those days.

When she gave birth 6 weeks early and in a massive emergent panic on Jan 25, 1997, I held my breath and waited. All I wanted was for her to live. I didn't think beyond that, I didn't hope beyond that.

A year later, I'm sitting beside her bed again, watching each breath with the rise and fall of her chest, listening for soft sighs or any noise that might tell me how, in the deepest of sleep, she feels. The difference this year is that I am not bracing myself for the worst, I don't expect to hear moans of pain or for her eyes to fly open in wild fear. I see, whether in my mind's eye or reality, a very slight smile playing on her lips. Sheer exhaustion will keep the woman from waking and seeing me watch her, or hearing the click of keys being pecked at as I type.

For the duration of our marriage, in between babies and dogs and in laws coming and going, the woman has worked determinedly towards honing her own martial arts skills and education. With no dojang to attend, she worked and sweated with TK Scott, adding his skills to the foundations of defense with which Uncle Sam had so graciously endowed her. Five out of six evenings were spent in intense training with him; when she could no longer train at a high level because of her pregnancy with our first child, she continued to exercise within the limits set by her physician. When our son was little more than a month old, she returned to the same energetic work-outs, challenging TK's ability to keep up with her.

Her only setback came 3 months into her pregnancy with our second child, our daughter. Warned of the risk, she took two steps back, inhaled a deep breath, and set the training aside. And she vowed she would return.

One year ago tonight, I never would have thought it possible.

Women, my father has told me often throughout my life, will always do what you least expect, they will find a will stronger than you can imagine, and they will overwhelm you with their compassion, their innate abilities, and their deep reserves of strength. My father was so very right. I would not have believed anyone could have come through teetering so close to the brink of life, all the time focusing on those around them without much concern for the precariousness of their own life, and still come back fighting stronger than ever.

The woman did not give up. And she did return to her training regimen. Within 9 weeks of giving birth—in an emergency situation requiring a cesarean—she was back in uniform and training with TK, this time on the floor of a new dojang, surrounded by unfamiliar faces and obvious anti-female bias on the part of many male students who joined after years of training under other instructors. She was the only female in the dojang with high intermediate skills. In very little time, she became the only female with advanced skills. Men who scoffed at training with her, and fighting with her, learned to respect her skills and determination, and to fear her ferocity in the ring. They learned the woman does not respect belittlement, and demands to be pushed as hard and fought as hard as they themselves would choose to be.

At 7am this morning, January 10, 1998, along with 5 men, the woman slipped into running shoes and began pacing herself for a 5 mile run. When they all crossed the finish line, she headed with them to the weight room for an hour of light weight training, and then joined them as they participated in all 4 Saturday morning classes. When the last class was over she assembled with the 5 men to begin the crux of the day—their black belt test, headed by my instructor, David Rodrigues, and his own instructor, Soon Mi Yi. After surviving what had already been a long day, they were put through their paces, physically tested on every concept and technique they could recall from the very basics to new forms taught just days before.

In the end, when the last kihap was bellowed and with sweat running in rivers, the woman stood with 3 men. There was no question in mind—she had been successful beyond my wildest dreams, and in my wildest dreams this woman has more talent than any human alive. It was not my call, however. By choice I did not sit on this testing panel. By my instructor's tradition, belts are awarded by order of score. I watched as my instructor placed belts around the waists of 3 male students who had garnered much of their training elsewhere; each had previously had very good, incredibly competent instructors. I swallowed hard; she stood last, she scored highest. By tradition, Soon Mi Yi would wrap a black belt around the waist of my wife.

Because she is my wife, Master Yi beckoned for me to stand with him. And because he is a gentleman of high caliber, knowing a great deal of what the woman had gone through to get to this day, Master Yi unfolded this belt, handed one end to me, and asked me to join him in awarding my wife her rank. When the final knot was tied, he took one end of the belt, I took the other, and together we gave it the final tug.

A year ago the woman was a heartbeat away from being gone from my life. Today I had the honor of watching her spread her wings and fly. I had the privilege of being there as her two young children, one running as fast as he could, and one taking two steps and falling, taking two more steps and falling, came from their places beside their grandfathers enveloped her in hugs and kisses. Like those two young souls, the woman took baby steps, then running strides, and then giant leaps to reach her goal.

What a difference a year makes.

THE BRICK WALL
When Do You Discipline—When Is It NOYB

The students who walk through our doors everyday have something in common aside from their desire to train, and to learn. They are human. And being human, they are given to human frailties and the tendency to make mistakes. When there are children involved, we're often asked to aid bewildered parents to helping a child navigate the right path. Finding that line that you should not cross over can be a tricky thing. Once you do find it, knowing how to step over it can be like banging your head into a brick wall.

How to handle student conduct outside the dojang can be a sticky situation. My first line of action is always to consult a student's parents in regards to any concerns I have about their behavior. Since this is their child, not mine, I believe my first responsibility is to make them aware of what I know regarding their child and allow them to remedy it in the manner they see fit. I also think it's important to verify the information; too often one or two kids will out and out lie about another over whom they carry a grudge. It would be unfair to act against a child unjustly accused.

Based on the parent's choice, presuming I have been therefore asked to intervene and help the situation by the parents, I will set aside private time to have a one-on-one discussion with a student. Many times just knowing the instructor is aware of outside behavior is enough to issue a wake-up call to a child displaying borderline behavior. I witnessed several times young students mortified when my own instructor questioned their actions outside class; what they believe to be private and harmless can quickly become embarrassing—and a lesson learned.

Simply asking a child if he knows how it feels to be on the receiving end of bullying—when they are not habitual bullies—makes them start to think and consider the consequences of their actions. When they are aware of what the long-term ramifications can be for the victim of their harassment—that it really does hurt beyond the moment escapes some children—they are less willing to repeat the behavior. Initially I think I would talk with the child, make him understand that I am aware of the situation, and that I disapprove immensely, and suggest ramifications if the behavior doesn't cease: I *will* dismiss a student from instruction if need be, or suspend them for a time (based on what the parent feels is the best course of action), and although I have not yet had to do so, I don't believe I would hesitate to suspend a student's rank.

While not something that would work with an adult student, temporary demotion for extreme situations does work with children and younger teens. It requires cooperation of the parents to assure that their child will continue to come to class—and participate as a lower ranked student—and in meeting behavior standards when they are allowed to resume their rank they are generally much more humble.

The first line for me, though, is the parents. As a parent myself I would not only want to be aware of this type of situation, but I would demand a hand in the resulting discipline. And as a parent, with a child actively training, I believe I would want cooperation from the child's instructor, insomuch as the skills this child has could go beyond mental and verbal harassment. I would do everything I could to hold onto the student (like it or not we are their best role models in control of the skills and emotions that result from training) and would only resort to dismissal from training as a last result.

It is a sticky situation. The adolescents are the ones who derive, even indirectly, the most from the examples we set for them, and as their instructors, I believe they do listen closely to what we say, how closely we follow our own advice, and how much we show we care. The chance is this child *will* listen to an instructor, and will make an attempt to rectify his own behavior—but he has to be given that chance first.

We cannot undermine and override a parent's wishes and methods of discipline. But we can be there when asked, and act when needed.

Breaking The Link

There is something to be said for the relationship forged between and instructor and student. We all go through life making friends and acquaintances; throughout our years in school we bounce from one teacher to the next, some make lasting impressions that change the course of your life, some instill fear, and some you just forget.

When you train in a martial art, you begin a relationship with the person who is teaching you. It can be wrought from a deep respect, chilling fear, admiration, camaraderie, or just the buckets of sweat put into the hours spent trying to grasp what is being taught.

If you spend enough years training under one particular instructor, the relationship becomes an extension of yourself. You take certain things for granted. Your expectation becomes, even on a subconscious level, that this is a relationship for life. It is not a neatly compact, this-is-my-home-life and this-is-my-training-life deal; those begin to overlap.

Unfortunately, familiarity can breed contempt.

I have had, over the years, a very close but very rocky relationship with my instructor. His skill is incredible, his heart large, and his compassion runs deep. He is still very closely associated with his own instructor of over 35 years. I often disagree with his ideas, and sometimes those disagreements were strong enough to cause me to step away from the training to take a good, hard look at what I was doing, and why. One was strong enough that I made the decision to step out his dojang and train on my own, and with my friend Dack Hunter, himself a 5th degree black belt. I always maintained contact with my instructor, openly sought his input, and tested under him.

When TK, Dack, and I made the decision to open a dojang we all felt it best to align ourselves with TK's and my instructor; we did not want to affiliate with a national organization, but felt it best to have ties to a well established, talented, willing mentor. He came with ties to a high ranking master instructor and was willing to travel to help us with black belt testing.

But, as I said, we have not always agreed on protocol. While his approaches have benefited me most of all, I have finally reached the point I am unwilling to continue in what some would consider a bastardization of the testing and promotion process; while I am by far a traditionalist, I do believe in setting and maintaining certain standards.

Many of you already know I was quite uneasy about testing for my 3rd degree black belt. While technically ready for it in physical terms, and I also believe in terms of skill, I felt it was inappropriate to offer me the opportunity to test when I did. On the basis of advice from friends long established in the martial arts, I went ahead and tested. I accepted the testing, as was advised, as my instructor's gift to me. It was by no means a given; I tested before a board that he was not a part of, comprised of people who did not know me.

Still, I have felt vaguely uneasy about it since.

In January our dojang held its first black belt testing, and as expected, my instructor made the trip to sit as head of the testing panel. I let him know in no uncertain terms that because my wife was testing, I would not be a part of the panel. I would participate as a pacer, going through each step of the test with the black belt candidates as a yardstick by which they could judge for themselves how much was expected, how much more than they had thought would be required of them actually was.

I was not prepared for his own instructor to tag along. And while I welcomed the surprise, I was certainly not expecting to find myself thrust onto the floor when the black belt candidates had finished and had been awarded rank to be further tested myself.

There exists, I believe, a valid reason for the general time period between testing for degrees of black belt. To be honest, I can't begin to reasonably articulate those reasons, but my gut tells me the waiting period is important. To have that ignored not once, but twice, bothered me a great deal. And it still does.

When asked about my rank, it was with great reluctance that I admitted to having been awarded third dan. When asked now, I prefer to not answer. Did I accept the rank when awarded? Yes, I did. It doesn't matter one way or the other within my own dojang what my rank is; it's a piece of paper and a strip of cloth with just one more stripe added. But I am not proud of how I have achieved my rank.

When you can't feel pride in accomplishments, when you feel shame over having something that most likely would have been yours simply with additional time, it's time to re-examine certain things. In this case I, along with my partners, needed to re-examine our continued affiliation with my instructor. I feel pride in the accomplishments of my students, in their efforts, but every time I strap that belt around my waist I feel a tinge of shame, and I feel like a fraud.

Often enough, it is said that rank is a subjective thing, in the end it amounts to a belt tied around the waist and a piece of paper hanging on the wall. For the most part, I agree with that whole heartedly; it was a very, very long time after testing for 3rd dan that I would even think of wearing the belt. And now…now I find excuses to not wear my rank even when teaching. It makes me feel like a fraud.

Because of this, which is most likely just the final element in a long like of catalysts, we have chosen to discontinue the affiliation. Dack is fond of quoting "lead by example," and if I can't show the same patience and put in the same sweat equity towards rank that I demand of my students and expect from my peers, then it becomes meaningless and degrades the honesty I feel I owe my students.

While I don't want them to worship the belt and chase the rank, I would hope that they have some respect for the process and what it takes to get far. Had we maintained that affiliation, I would have been asking one thing of them while demonstrating another.

It's not until you have to cut those ties that you realize how strong they really were. I am confident we did the right thing, but I feel some regrets, and a quantitative amount of sadness. In the end it will make us a better school, a more honest school.

I owe my instructor much. I owe my students more. There's an old saying "A chain is only as strong as its weakest link." Caught in the middle, the link had to be broken. With hope and more hard work, the chain will be whole once again. Perhaps then, I'll feel like less of a fraud.

The Balance Of Life

Imagine, if from the very first moment that you took up a martial art and began training in earnest, that you never failed. Everything shown to you comes easily, as though it were already an integral part of your being, and it requires no effort to accomplish, only the sweat that comes with physically moving your body from point A to point B. You remember, subconsciously, all you are shown; if someone barks *Chosan* or *Sam Il* or *Unsu* you can perform the poomse or kata flawlessly. A static jump reverse double inside-outside crescent kick doesn't faze you in the least. The training requires such little effort that you breeze through from day one until your coveted black belt test in less than 2 years. You're nothing short of a prodigy.

So there you are, wearing a crisp, brand new black belt, left in charge of a room full of new students, and you're showing them how to get from the first technique in a form to the next, when some brave soul asks "Why? Why do we do that?" and you don't really know. *You* do it because it's what you were shown to do. It's what you are able to do without much conscious thought. The block precedes the punch which precedes the kick—what more do you need to know?

No one particularly likes it when bad things happen to them. Most people would rather go through life without being touched by illness or death; we would all prefer that those marriage vows we took in good faith remain as strong as was the intent behind them, no one wants to lose a job or fail an exam, there isn't a soul amongst us who would enjoy being told "I just don't love you, so goodbye."

The human instinct is to find the things that make life pleasant. We gravitate towards the things that interest us, that make our lives more peaceful and more pleasant. We avoid the pitfalls along the way, and strive to be as happy as we possibly can. Some of subconsciously venture out onto paths that are inevitably contrary to our happiness and well being, but the shadows that lurk there aren't so obvious from the outset. The goal is evident: don't worry, be happy.

Still, if you have never failed, how do you measure your success? If you have never felt ill, where does your yardstick to measure your health begin? If you have never felt sad, how do you know if you're happy?

About 5 years ago, after 10 years of marriage, my first wife decided that for whatever reason (there were several, to be sure) it just wasn't working, and it was time to end the relationship as we knew it. This wasn't easy; we had been a couple since the very beginnings of puberty. I was content in the relationship, at least I thought I was. I never harbored any thoughts of leaving, or seeing any other women. I made the commitment and I intended to stick by it. My wife, on the other hand, saw what I did not: long, frequent business trips, restlessness, weekends buried in paperwork that could have waited. She made the painful decision. She left. She took a chance for both of us and changed forever what had been intended to be a life long union.

Yes, it was painful. And I was angry for a time, mostly at myself for failing to recognize the truth. Yet not too long afterwards someone else entered my life, and changed my perceptions entirely. My sense of self soared; I realized then that contentment and happiness are not one and the same. You can be utterly content with spaghetti for dinner every night, but it's not necessarily healthy. By stepping outside the confinements of what I thought was happiness, I found the real thing. It was worth the pain, and it was worth the confusion of letting go of things in the past (and for the nosey, yes, I remain friends with my ex-wife, and wish her nothing but happiness with her new husband and six stepkids).

Last year, at what I thought was the apex of good health, I crashed and burned. I had a heart attack. My perception of healthy changed drastically. I had low body fat, low cholesterol, I ate well, none of the markers for potential cardiac problems. I exercised.

Surprise, surprise.

Earlier this year, without any real prep time, or warning, and without the benefit of Time in Training that should not have been ignored, I entered a rank test and passed. Did that make me happy I could advance quickly or proud of the accomplishment? Not in the least. Contrarily, it disappointed and upset me. It lacked balance.

There exists real reasons for the stumbling blocks of life. Call it the yin and yang of personal existence. When a life ends, it is profoundly sad; when a life begins, it is intensely joyous. When one relationship ends, it hurts; when a new one enters your life, it brings back the excitement of living, and when it clicks well, it's intense. When the rank test you were sure was yours for just showing up doesn't yield the results you expect, it isn't a failure; it's an opportunity to glean from the experience the little things you missed the first time.

If everything in your training comes to you without effort, with such ease that you never have to question why—or you can't answer someone else's "why?", then it's time to pry the proverbial coin up off the floor and flip it over to get a really good look at the other side. Nothing worthwhile should come without a price, at least not without effort. If you breeze from point to point without any self doubts, or questions about efficiency of your art, or its applicability, then something is wrong. You can't have total success without a measure of at least doubt if not occasional failure.

The balance of life touches everything.

Between Bullets and Tears

"...so what happens is that some boys can't cry tears. They cry bullets." William Pollack, author of <u>*Real Boys: Rescuing Our Sons From The Myths Of Boyhood.*</u>

Big boys don't cry.
Act your age—be a man.
Don't be a sissy, fight back.
Just don't cry!

One of the rules for underbelt sparring in our dojang is that no face contact is allowed. At brown belt, adults may engage in light face contact by mutual consent; kids, however, are encouraged to avoid making contact with their sparring partner's face. The risks of permanent damage outweigh any training benefit derived from making face contact, so in the interest of our student's long term health and well being, it becomes one of the first rules they learn.

A few nights ago I watched two young students, one 7 years old, the other 9, both beginners, square off in the ring. Both boys, both free of fear, both eager to strut their stuff and show just how good they were, how tough and unbeatable. A little over a minute into the match, which was little more than two wild men swinging at air, the younger of the two made solid contact with the other's nose. It was a sick sounding, dull thud that stopped them both in their tracks. The older boy immediately covered his nose with his hand and stared in total astonishment. The younger boy burst into tears.

It only took an instant to soak in the reactions of the students present; males in their teens and early twenties grimaced, but made a determined effort to not watch the young boy crying distraught tears over having hurt someone. They obviously felt a certain amount of empathy for the young man holding his bruised nose in hand, but the look was clear: whatever you do, don't cry. And he knew his lesson well, he shook it off and was ready to resume fighting.

I ended the match and sent him off the floor to get an icebag from the freezer; my wife drew the younger boy aside to console him and explain that no one was seriously hurt, nothing that a good apology couldn't fix.

It occurs to me now that in 2 more years, perhaps 3, the younger of the two boys will have developed that wall that most males do, and he'll be able to hold back the emotion, choke off the tears, and blow the whole thing off with a machismo-laden "you're ok, let's keep going."

My son will be 3 years old in September. He's a very determined creature, free-spirited, and unencumbered by what he perceives as the expectations of society. He has a caring soul, loves openly and without hesitation or reservation, and cries if he's hurt. He cries just as hard when someone else is hurt. His baby sister, just 18 months old, bumped her head on the bottom of the table; he raced to hug her, kiss the owie, and used the situation to sucker Mom for cookies for the both of them. He has no notion that his gentleness and freedom to express his emotions will someday be seen as unmasculine. He expresses what he feels when he feels it.

In time, he will learn to hide his feelings. He'll adopt the mask of masculinity, he'll toughen himself against the things that hurt him, he'll learn to choke back tears, to swallow them, until they no longer flow easily. He'll become the 9 year old in the ring, astonished at sudden pain, but unwilling to display an outward appearance of it.

And that saddens me.

I'm not an advocate of Tears in Training. I see no useful purpose in actively encouraging students of either gender to cry when it hurts; it is going to hurt, and it will hurt often. But the shame I saw drawn in the faces of other males present almost astonished me. I had forgotten The Code; I had let slip the details of growing into manhood, the unwritten rules that say you must not cry, you swallow it whole, but you do not cry.

Part of being male is aggression; testosterone alone makes men more aggressive than women. Part of aggression is anger, and part of training is learning to control anger before it controls you, before it clouds your mind and turns a situation where you may need to defend yourself or someone you care about into a situation of uncontrolled confusion. There's still that part inside that no matter the training, in spite of years of sweating to gain control of yourself, that refuses to let go. We let the dictates of society determine how we express ourselves, and when you can't express sorrow in tears, or joy, or tears of abject astonishment , it has to go somewhere. For some it becomes rage that feeds upon itself.

These are the boys who cry bullets instead of tears. The boys who, without any other direction or understanding of how to channel their feelings, harden that mask of masculinity and turn to violence. They are no longer capable of venting sorrow or frustration the way they did when they were small. No one has ever given them any other options. The message has been pounded into them through every available avenue: be tough, be strong, don't wimp out, don't let anyone step on you, and don't cry.

How many pre-adolescent and teenage males in your schools are encroaching into the gray area between understanding their feelings, how to express them, when to hold them back, and when it's ok to show them?

I had the opportunity to make a small dent in the testosterone armor and I did not take it.

Hindsight tells me now that I very easily could have been the one to step into the ring and comfort both boys; though only one was crying, I know well enough to realize the older boy was only practicing what he had learned would serve him well. I instead relied on stereotype: I let a woman address the tears, and I sent off a 9 year old to stoically handle his own pain. It's what's expected.

It's not what is right.

Like it or not, we are role models for our students; male instructors have the golden opportunity to be for their young male students an example of what a man can be. We don't always have to be tough, we don't always have to hide behind the masks we learned to wear so well as children. We can be gentle, we can scoop up a crying child and give comfort; we can, through our own example, let them see that real men can be tender, real men do have feelings, and real men display them without being wimps.

It's a major task to cut through the stereotypes we've woven around ourselves throughout life; in a place intended to train people to fight, and to fight hard, tenderness is very nearly an anomaly. This is a chance, however, for our male students to witness something they may never get elsewhere, to learn something very subtly they cannot get from the myriad of action movies and cable TV they watch; they can learn that this toughness is only a small part of who we are. No matter how skilled and tough in the ring, how well we can fight, they can learn from us the skills to cope with the emotions they've fought to bite down on.

Sometimes big boys do cry.

Amazing Grace

The first time I saw Justin Simms he was three years old. He lived in a 4 bedroom house with 14 relatives, slept on a twin mattress on the floor of his cousins' bedroom, played contentedly in the kitchen, on the floor, which was located near the back of the house—the "safe place." He did not dare venture outside to play in the yard, could not fathom the idea of a swing set or sandbox, and the grass out front was only something the neighbor's untrained, ill-kept dog used as a repository for personal waste.

Justin's world was inside that house; unlike most of the houses in his neighborhood—a place he rarely saw—his was a home. He lived without fear and was protected by a large family who dreamed mostly of Justin growing up and growing away from the neighborhood. They had, after all, managed to raise two young girls into womanhood, safe and unscathed by the turmoil around them, and had seen them into college and a successful government career. With the same guidance, Justin could escape the grip of the city gangs; he would be somebody.

I was an anomaly to Justin. His only vision of white people was through the television screen, and although only three, he was keenly aware that what he saw emanating from that box was not real; nothing there had a viable connection to his own reality. When I walked through the door, he had his first face-to-face contact with a white man; being three, he was not shy about exploring his curiosities.

It took him a very long time to believe that my skin was real skin; he lifted my shirt, studied my chest, looked at my back. He even lifted my pants legs and pulled down my socks, checking everything he could to see if this strange person was white all over. And when he was done, he just smiled and told me I was "funny lookin'." There was no judgment there, no preconceived notions about who I should be or how I should act. Justin was his own world of innocence and opinion, and as long as I was willing to get down on the floor and play with his cars with him, and as long as I did not mind reading the same story to him countless times, I could be his friend. I fell in love with this little boy, and if I could have, I would have taken him home with me then and there.

The next time I saw Justin Simms he was 6 and a half years old. He was quiet, unmoving, twisting the handle of a vinyl gym bag around his fingers, unwilling to look up and meet the eyes of anyone in the room. Still years away from adolescence, his eyes had the tired, worn look of someone old, and he carried himself with an air of distrust. He had not forgotten me; we spoke often on the phone, he remembered Christmas and birthday gifts that came without fail, and reminded me that I was still "funny lookin'." Still, he refused to approach me with the same abandon he has as a curious toddler.

He eyed the swing set in the side yard with suspicion; he sat at the edge of the sandbox in the front yard tensely, watching his younger cousins play, but held back from actual participation. He looked up occasionally to take in the surroundings of trees and blue sky, and watched in unbridled amazement as birds flocked to a feeder stand, and as rabbits hopped confidently past the garden. What he did not do, something that should be as natural as breathing to a six year old, was play.

For the first time in his young life, he had his own room; his bed was not a mattress thrown on the floor, but a full bed. His room was ready for a boy to destroy in the way that kids do, a bookcase waiting to be filled, a toy box stocked with typical little boy cars and Legos, with room for whatever else his young heart would want. He touched none of it. Instead he sat close by as the adults talked, he absorbed every word, watched every nuance. There was no little boy there any longer, and I wanted to know what had happened to Justin Simms.

His uncle stated it simply and succinctly: "He went outside."

Brad Simms has been, for all of his own children's lives, the force that kept the family together. While at questionable odds with the way he made a living to support them, he made sure his house was filled with love, rules, and more love. He pushed education as a value he would not permit to be belittled; he instilled in his family a deep abiding faith that if they did what was right, worked hard enough, and stayed away from those he had no choice but to deal with, they could rise above their own circumstances and be better than society wanted them to be.

His youngest nephew was no exception. He wanted for this boy the things his own children had been able to make for themselves: advanced education, careers, and families that did not have to hide in houses with barred windows. He wanted the child to have a life where the sound of a bang meant someone's car was backfiring, not that someone one street over was being shot. He was, however, not Justin's father, and when Justin was 5 years old, his mother moved from their house, and took her son along.

Justin went outside, and he was never the same.

I have never pressed Brad Simms for the details of his life in the neighborhood in which he raised his two daughters. It was always enough for me that he loved his children more than his own life, that he treated them with respect and honor, and that he wanted for life to better for them than it had ever been for himself. When Justin's mother moved out, with the rest of his family old enough to make their own life decisions, Brad left his home and moved to be closer to his oldest daughter and his grandchildren. He kept contact with his sister and exerted as much influence as he could over his young nephew's life, but with the miles between them and the realities of life in an inner city neighborhood, his influence was diluted. When Justin's mother realized her little boy no longer felt safe, when he knew things that no child should ever know and had seen things most adults never will, she made the most painful decision of her own life: she packed up what few things he owned, and sent him to live with his uncle.

I wanted, though, to know what had happened to transform Justin from the curious, outgoing, happy toddler I first knew, to the quiet, seriously tense little boy who stared at this family of virtual strangers with suspicion and trepidation. His curiosity hadn't vanished, I could see that much from the occasional light that popped out when he watched wild animals venture out from the woods behind our house, or when he realized his baby cousin was doing something for the very first time. It was kept in check, reigned in tightly. He no longer felt free enough to explore.

After weeks of quiet adjustment to his new surroundings, Brad brought Justin to the dojang. Ostensibly, it was to show him where his older cousin, Brad's daughter, disappeared to every afternoon, but we all also wanted to see if it would spark some interest in him. He watched for a while, shrugged and said in no uncertain terms "I can do any of that. I don't need no lessons."

Let onto the floor with protective gear and the freedom to try, Justin came at me wildly, kicking and hitting, with a keen instinct for what would hurt the most. Had I been another 6 year old boy, I would have been seriously hurt. He fought as if he meant it, and yet he soaked in every detail about his surroundings. He stopped swinging long enough to ask about flowers he had seen in a vase on the front desk.

"Who died?" When assured no one had, he balked. "Flowers are for dead people. They get shot and die, and then you put flowers down where they got shot." When asked if he had ever witnessed a shooting, he looked at me as if I had asked the most inane question possible. Everyone, he knows, has seen another person shot dead in the middle of the street. It's just the way it is. You don't even have to see it happen to know if the dead was young or old, male or female. All you need is to see what is there on the street the next day; flowers and ribbons, or teddy bears for the very young. Candles and crosses sometimes.

"You know," he tells me earnestly and without a trace of disgust, "when dead people lay there a long time, they get hard."

Over the next few weeks, while summer slid by and Justin came to the dojang to "fight the old man" he began to relax and began to talk more. At six and a half he has seen more than anyone ever should. He can tell you what a prostitute is, where to go in his neighborhood to see the rubber tree, a secluded spot in a park where used condoms litter the ground; he knows that a magazine is not always something you read, but a clip in which bullets go. He knows, too, that had he stayed with his mother, he would "be like everyone," and die before he turns 21.

Justin Simms has lived through the stereotype of urban childhood, he is proof in the flesh that the world in which my wife grew up but does not speak of exists. He is a testament to my father-in-law's wisdom and courage in remaining in that environment to be a positive influence on youth. He is a young soul still able to grow the wings he will need to soar, he can rise above the brief time he spent surviving there. He is luckier than most: the boys with whom he plodded through kindergarten will not be so lucky. More than half will wind up in gangs. Some will die before they hit puberty. Most will live in poverty and suffer the slings of racism.

Every single one of the students who have come through our dojang door has done so for a reason. Yet I would bet real money that none has seen the realities of Justin's life; in seeking to learn to protect themselves they are guided by the ghosts of media violence as seen on television, whispered stories they hear of what happened to someone else. Some have experience real brutality and choose to prepare themselves for the possibility it may happen again. Yet none have lived it on a consistent, day to day basis, and none assume that bodies on the street are a simple fact of life, and that flowers are only for the dead.

There is a grace in surviving the horrors of life. When it means escaping the rings of violence, bypassing the lure of drugs and the easy money they bring, coming to understand that sex is something you share and not something you purchase, that there is a dignity of self that is a person's right and not something to be given or taken away, it is incredible. I can teach my students to defend themselves, I can teach them to avoid situations that present real physical danger, but I cannot teach them the things that a hard life can place at their feet. That a six year old can look into the bowels of life and not lose himself to disgust, but emerge intact and with more grace than most adults have in a lifetime, it is more than just impressive. It is amazing.

Bang Bang You're Dead

I should make it clear up front that I own a gun. Several, in fact. I am licensed to carry a concealed weapon and if you plop me down on a target range and pop up a very small target I will probably hit the center or it 9 out of 10 times. I can hit moving targets, static targets, full body outlines or things smaller than a playing card zooming by at fairly high speeds. I have spent countless hours developing my skills, mostly out of necessity, partially out of ego. I am not anti-gun.

But, I will say this: if you use a gun as an offensive weapon, you are nothing more than a coward.

We all grow up playing cops and robbers, pointing our index fingers at each other and screaming "BANG! You're dead!" and we all took our turns at melodramatic death, clutching our chests and wailing loudly as we slowly dropped to the ground in a convulsive fit. It was funny, it was cool, it was nothing but play-acting, and it was a time in our young lives when death had not yet touched the fabric of our beings, and the surrealism of the play had nothing to do with the realities of life. We played a violent game with pacifistic hearts, we took our turns at being dead and we took our turns at pointing fingers and shooting our friends, but when dusk settled we all got up, said goodbye, and went home.

The chance that any of us had ever seen with our own young eyes a *real* gun was slim at best; my father was a police officer, and I vaguely recall catching a glimpse of his sidearm once, other than when it was holstered as part of his uniform, but other than that glimpse, it was kept well hidden from my curious eyes. Several of us owned bright shiny plastic replicas of cop guns, or if you were really cool, you had a metal cap gun that barely worked, but real guns were beyond our comprehension; we knew they existed and what they did, but we didn't think much about it, because those were for grownups and not for kids. They were for cops, and maybe hunters—although we were all sure hunters did not use handguns, they used rifles, and they came home with more stories than dead animals.

Today the average 5 year old knows what a gun is and that its a weapon intended as use to kill people. Not that its something a cop has, or maybe a hunter: it's a weapon for use in killing people. Bad guys have them and shoot people they don't like. Cops have them and shoot bad guys. Mom has one in case someone breaks in, and she says she'll kill anyone who comes near her.

It's as easy as being a patient soul to get a gun now. Go to the store, pay for it, wait 5 to 10 to 15 days depending on the state in which you live, and the gun is yours to take home. You don't have to have special training, you don't have to prove you know how to clean it without killing the kid in the next room, you just have to pay and wait. No one is required to tell you that if you intend to use this gun for self defense purposes, you're more likely to get killed with it because you choked and had it taken away from you, and then used on you. Just pay and wait.

My 11 year old nephew knows that somewhere in my house, is a safe with at least 2 guns that he knows of. He also knows that if I ever catch him purposely looking for it, he'll be banned from my house for quite a while. If I were to ever catch him with so much as a finger on my gun, or any other gun, I would probably do something I have never done to a child; I would probably whack him one. His older brothers also know that somewhere in the house my guns are locked away, but they've reached the age where they either don't care, or just plain know better. The difference between them, and the difference between me at their ages, is the loss of innocence. Not only are they acutely aware of weapons and functions, they have had more than a glimpse of the real thing. They have all held a gun, pointed a gun, and fired a gun. They know the smell of a spent shell, the power of recoil. The know that a hole blasted through a paper target equates a hole in a body. An injury. A potentially fatal wound.

They graduated from playground games of cobs and robbers, using their fingers as the weapon, to standing in a cold firing range with an uncle bent on making sure they learned the power of the gun, to handle one correctly, and that the weapon they hold in their hands is not the innocuous necessity their chosen entertainment venues make it out to be. You don't shoot someone and have them spring back to life in the sequel. You don't pull a weapon on someone and count on there being an empty chamber for the sake of drama. You can't shoot and then expect to put a quarter back in the slot and start all over. They need to know now, while their opinions are being formed by experience, that it is not a toy. It is real. And it can kill them.

There are no weapons in TaeKwonDo. It is an empty hand art; you fight with your hands, you fight with your feet;

your opponents, on the other hand, might very well be armed with a weapon. I have heard from several students already that they see no value in learning to use a gun as part of their training; they came to me to learn to defend themselves with the weapons God graced them with, and nothing more.

Whatever God graced them with, it was not the innate knowledge of what to do when staring down the barrel of a gun, nor how that gun will react when the person holding it is kicked, or grabbed. God didn't plant seeds of wisdom that will help even the most physically talented martial artist to keep from inadvertently redirecting the fire of that gun towards an innocent bystander. God may have given them all weapons in the guise of hands and feet and heads, but he also gave them brains.

I am not advocating that every person out there with aspirations in the martial arts rush out and join the NRA (for those politically oriented, no, I am not a member either). I *do* strongly advocate that as part of defense training the very basics of handling and firing guns be learned from a trained professional. In a nation where the right to bear arms is constitutional law, more and more people are opting to do so—and many of them are the bad guys—the people who would seek out to cause you deliberate harm.

The times when we stood in our yards and pointed innocent fingers at one another, chanting "Bang bang, you're dead, fifty bullets in your head" is long gone. The guns are real; the bullets are real. In our grown up world, so should be our education. It does not shortchange ones' martial arts training to admit that guns should be a part of it; it can enhance it. Whether you ever choose to own a handgun or not, the odds favor you more if you know the full potential of a weapon.

Test? Why A Test?

Testing can be a pain in the butt. It's high stress for the students and time consuming for the instructors. Most students are aware of their progress in relationship to the school's curriculum and an instructor doesn't arbitrarily assign students to a testing date—presumably he already knows who is ready and who is not.

So why schedule testing dates that take up so much time and stress out the students?

It's the Power Of The Deadline.

Deadlines are a motivator that produce results. They get you going, get you focused, and get you to put just that little extra oomph into training. You might be "good enough" to pass the test before you know the date is scheduled, and you might be theoretically ready to progress to the next level, but in focusing on improving your basic foundations to pass this dreaded exam, you just might exceed expectations and improve past the point of 'just passing' the test. You may break past a personal barrier, become more physically fit, and find reserves of energy and strength you did know that you had.

That stress felt by a looming test isn't necessarily a bad thing. It means you feel the pressure and you want to succeed; that you recognize progress isn't just going to fall into your lap. No one is going to pat you on the head and murmur "good kid...you showed up, so here's a reward" and then just hand over that rank belt. You *know* you have to earn it, and only you can put forth the effort required to get there.

People are capable, generally, of much more than they usually think they are. They see pressure and stress as an obstacle and not a motivational tool. It doesn't have to be that way. Weddings are stressful, yet we welcome the stress as excitement; the ceremony reminds us to be better people for the sake of the person to whom we are committing ourselves. Childbirth is stressful, yet we willingly undertake it because we know that the end result is well worth the anxiety over totally changing a lifestyle. There is nothing more stressful than seeing someone you deeply love in real danger, and the stress is incredible, yet time after time you hear stories of someone overcoming the stress and using it to save someone—a child trapped in water under ice; a husband trapped under the wheel of a car and whose wife uses sheer gut power to lift the vehicle; this is stress at its ultimate. This is people harnessing that stress and making it work.

Sudden stress is something you either deal with and make it work, or fail to deal with and flounder. When that rank test is looming, you have time on your side, you can make a deliberate choice to face it head on and greet it as a motivating factor in your training, or you can fear it and back away. That you may have questions regarding your abilities and whether or not you deserve to promote are natural; self doubt is a human thing and it means you're aware that you are not perfect and there is room for improvement. The mere fact that you are being scheduled to test suggests that your instructor is aware that you are, indeed, ready; you have this chance to better the test, you have this as the chance to perform beyond your own expectations.

That upcoming test is your deadline; it's your signal that you only have so much time to meet certain standards, and while you probably already do, it's time to prove it. The deadline can motivate you or make you freeze with fear.

The choice is yours.

Happy Holidays

It started with the first snowflakes and the sound of two newborn babies wailing in the background. Generally once the first bite of winter starts nipping, I turn into a six foot three, one hundred eighty five pound kid; I know the holidays are close, and it's my favorite time of year. I love the decorations and all the food, I don't mind the crowds in malls, and I love watching the little kids just stand there in total wonder. It's no different this year; as soon as I saw those first few flakes I started feeling like a little kid grown tall all over again. The difference is being jerked back into adulthood by the sound of newborn boys wailing to be fed and changed.

My partner, TK, and his wife Becky are the proud parents of new twin boys, William and Richard. They came into the world on November 11th, two very tiny but very loud gifts, bright reminders of the holiday season and all the things we have to be thankful for. Still, while the adult part of me was thinking in terms of the blessings these two new souls bring to us all, the kid in me is realizing here are 2 more reasons to spend a lot of time at Toys R Us.

Everyone likes to get presents; I happen to get a bigger kick out of giving them. By the end of December my

MasterCard will have suffered meltdown, and we'll sit back and wonder "didn't we say we wouldn't go overboard this year?" My wife will roll her eyes because she knows who the biggest kid in the house is. She won't complain, she understands the thrill I get out of finding the right gift for the right person.

This year our students are included; as a holiday gift each one will receive a new uniform. No one really needs one, and for the most part I don't care what a students shows up to class in as long as they're not naked and everything that legally should be covered is. I couldn't pass up the chance when presented with a design for a different kind of uniform based on surgical scrubs (thanks to Mike Thompson, husband of our Wayward Wabbit Thumper) By the end of December all our current students will have the chance to work out dressed in bright red, white, and blue; we'll look like the most patriotic dojang in this half of the century.

We owe a lot to our students; they help define who we are and how we relate to people. Students give us the chance to stretch our imaginations, looking for creative ways to teach them the skills they look to us for; just their presence gives us the chance to enhance our own abilities by digging deep down to understand and explain the fundamentals. While they often pay us for these services, and thanks us often, as instructors I'd say it's a safe bet we don't often thank them for being our students.

A gift to a student doesn't have to be a big thing; it doesn't have to be something material. This time of year many MA schools are celebrating the holidays with parties and outside activities; some are taking hayrides together, some are banding together to perform community service in the spirit of the holidays. In all the rush and excitement, it might not occur to any one of us to thank them for their dedication and hard work, and for giving us the opportunity to teach.

If you have a chance this year—and it's not too late—send each of your students a card with a personal note. Let them know that you do appreciate them, and are honored to be chosen as the one who will instruct them. A few kind words go a very long way, and will be remembered long after the toys and clothing and new uniforms are long forgotten.

When It's Not "Can I?" But "Will I?"

You are undoubtedly the best student in your school. You have a flair for technique; you have speed, timing, and you have dexterity. Your practice of forms is enviable; while you work hard at it and deep down you know that what makes it seem effortless is hundreds of hours of careful attention to the basics, others watch in admiration, because you make it seem so easy. New students aspire to your level of expertise. Most students want to partner with you, or be there when you teach a class, because you know your art backwards and forwards, and you have an innate sense of how to teach. Your own instructor marvels at your dedication to the art and your willingness to pass on what you know. You are, in every sense of the word, excellent at what you do.

But...can you defend yourself?

The issue has been raised before, whether or not proficiency in any given art will automatically give a practitioner the upper hand in an altercation; my experience with some very competent black belts over the last couple of years tells me that the training and the persistent quest for quality does not mean that one can adequately defend himself. Sometimes it's a matter of the way one was taught; their particular system might rely heavily on sport applications, or the school might take the road towards teaching a particular curriculum without regard for teaching the defense applications of those techniques in a manner that makes them immediately useful in a modern fight.

In the midst of all the different teaching methods available, and the drive to present a system which is more than adequate in terms of offering reliable self-protection and preservation of the fundamental roots of the art, there exist practitioners who excel at their art, who excel at teaching their art and making the information understandable, but who cannot use what they know in defense of themselves.

Over the years I have become acquainted with an individual who possesses incredible skill and has the ability to teach on levels I can only hope to attain. Technically her form is very good and her knowledge base sound, but when push comes to shove she will fold up into a tight little ball and start crying her eyes out. She *knows* how to defend herself, but her confidence, even through all her years of training, has been systematically eroded by an emotionally abusive father who systematically picked away at the layers of her self esteem and manipulated her into situations no child should ever face. The abuse is in the past, but she has not yet learned to accept herself and take as a part of her the confidence she has learned as a facade. In years of training, she has never felt worth defending, and has never given herself permission to defend.

With a good instructor, confidence comes with training; as you learn more, you become more aware of your surroundings, you know that you have the tools to deal with situations as they arise, and the confidence builds on itself. Knowing you have that power, even though in all likelihood you will never have to use it, notches your self esteem up a few more points. It becomes not instinctive, not in the sense that a mother would die to protect her child, but reactive. A punch comes flying at your nose and you've blocked it without thinking. You don't need to think; you react.

There are some things that even those who are ready to defend themselves cannot bring themselves to do—like poking someone's eye out. It's gross. It's irreversible. It's not something many people want to learn. They don't want to know that they can have someone choking to death on their own blood within seconds. They want to defend themselves, but don't wish to hurt someone in the process. This is where a person has to give himself permission; a person must know, deep down, that they are worth it, that if someone else cares so little about them as to attempt to cause intentional harm, then they have right to react to protect, even if that means truly, deeply injuring another human being in some very despicable ways.

Other defense techniques, throwing techniques, leg locks, wrist locks, those are the easy things to learn because they don't come with much baggage; you can learn those because you know that when you go to bed at night, the worst you would be doing is breaking an arm or a leg, something that with time will heal. When you get right down to it and know that what you do can blind someone forever, or have them gasping for breath through a larynx crushed beyond repair, have them choking to death on their own blood, you have to make the decision: "Am I worth it? Do I deserve to live more than this scum who is attacking me?"

Out in this world exists a high number of advanced black belts who would have to honestly answer no; deep down they *don't* think that their lives are worth more. they can perform all the necessary techniques and teach them well, but they can't carry through, and not from lack of ability or desire. Because of their personal foundations, they cannot give themselves the permission necessary to use all means needed when an altercation arises.

When you decide that your life is just as valuable as anyone else's, your reactions will allow you to defend yourself, even in the most distasteful ways if necessary. There is not a single person out there whose life is not valuable; get the reactive response needed. Give yourself permission to defend, and to live.

Gutting It Out

Thirteen people stand on the workout floor, ready to test. Several are physically gifted students who should be able to sail through the test without much difficulty. Two are students with well defined problems, one of them has never been able get more than two inches off the ground, and she probably never will. The other has physical disabilities which make many techniques impossible. All know the techniques and forms on which the test will be based; if not, they would not have been issued the invitation to test in the first place.

I've heard it whispered in moans in the locker room that testing is a waste of time; if we already know the students who are testing know the material, both mentally and physically, why don't we just give them the belt and move on? It can't be for the money—we don't charge for testing.

There's the Power Of The Deadline. It can push a student to work harder, break beyond any barriers they feel they have, some real, some imagined. It's tangible proof that the hard work pays off, that a prolonged moment of stress can be met with success. When you know something will not just be handed to you, but it must be earned, you'll work at it if you really want it.

In the effort, there lies the success.

All of our testings are open; students and family are free to come and observe. That doesn't mean, however, that observing previous tests will indicate to a student what he should expect. Testing protocol can change to suit the needs of the day; where one test might have seem relatively easy, another may not. While watching students warm up, we are still formulating the day's test.

So here we are, with thirteen students eager to start, and to get it over with. Most of them undoubtedly feel they have nothing to prove; they've done it all in class over and over. They've sparred, they've sweated through forms, they've done their time on the mat, throwing and being thrown, they've each demonstrated a measurable knowledge of self defense; when presented with a series of attacks, each is capable of offering more than one defense tactic as response. Some are better than others. Still, there is the possibility that more than one will leave the test disappointed; in spite of their abilities proven in class, they may not find success in this test.

Since this is an advanced rank test, all were cautioned to set aside a good portion of their day. Previous tests were merely a rehashing of curriculum, two hours at most, with the physical exertion required comparable to that of a good conditioning class. None had any reason to expect anything different when the test began; when the warm up ended nearly an hour later (which were not the familiar exercises they expected, but more of an aerobic class format), more than twice as long as the class norm, most began to suspect this would not be the cake walk they had hoped for; some began to expect it was the torture they had feared.

The grumbling began at the water fountain: "What does this have to do with the test? If I wanted to prance around I'd join a gym..."

The grumbling continued in the weight room, angry hushed groans of bewilderment; what in the world did weight training have to do with testing for a red belt or a brown belt?

While conspicuously ignoring those comments, we focused instead on the few who were not questioning motive, but doing everything asked of them, with the best effort they could put forth.

Nearly two hours later, when most expected this test to be over, it finally began in earnest. Tired and exhausted, they assembled back on the floor for forms. While some may have assumed that after all the previous sweating, we would require only the advanced forms, we began at day one, white belt basics. When taken through to the final form, our black belt form, all were offered the chance to step aside if they were unfamiliar with it; most chose the opportunity to rest, to catch their breath. Only five took the chance to try it, even though they had only seen it a few times and had been through it in class two or three times at most.

There were five different versions of the same form going on at the same time; the student who cannot get off the floor modified the form on the spot to suit her limitations and removed several jump kicks. The others simply did what they remembered and formulated the rest on their own. In spite of what was, by then, sheer exhaustion coming at them from every angle, and muscles burning with use, none of those five gave up. While they may not have known the form, the success was in the effort.

After the last sweat drenched punch, the remaining students lined up, fully expecting this was the end; hope, at least, was evident in their faces. Instead we dragged out the mats for defense drills. We attacked, they responded. We attacked harder; some put forth benign efforts that clearly said "I don't want to do this anymore." Some gave their best efforts, which, because of fatigue, were clearly less than their abilities, but their fire was not gone.

With the mats put away, the hope that this was over was obvious pleading in the eyes of most. I saw raw determination only in a few faces. In that determination, I also saw trust. These few knew that in spite of the torture, I would not push anyone to the real breaking point; I would not allow harm to come from this test.

I pulled out my sparring gear. Clear defeat blanketed several students when they realize that they would not be sparring with their equally fatigued testing partners, but that they would be sparring with me. Most of them ran around the ring, avoiding contact, avoiding looking at me directly. A few made obvious effort to fight back and defend. One, who knew I would not hit hard, made the attempt to distract me with cries of a sharp leg cramp; when I moved in to make sure she was all right, she kicked me square in the chest. Yes, I saw it coming. Yes, I could have blocked. Sometimes allowing the shot to come through is the right thing to do. She was not giving up. I could have kept her in that ring until she could no longer stand. She intended to fight until I said the fight was over.

She deserved that shot.

No, she cannot jump. She cannot spin well. Her balance is not perfect and her speed is not always good enough to close the distance. She does, however, have a keen sense of what she is doing, she knows her technique, she knows her forms inside and out, and she can differentiate between practical and show, and she can defend herself—but most importantly, *she does not quit.*

She had, at the onset of the test, hoped to leave as a first gup brown belt; she left as a black belt candidate. She may never possess the raw talent and sheer ability others have, but she has the tenacity of a black belt.

No one walked off the floor at any point and refused to continue; some put out more effort than others, but all did give what was, for them, a best effort. All passed, but some shined. They gutted it out past expectations, both their own and mine. The most physically talented student cannot match the gift of that determination. Most, I think, learned the value of the test that began with no martial arts meaning. What comes with ease is not always what is worth rewarding. What comes with effort and determination is.

Whose Time Is It Anyway?
...And Other things That Tick Me Off...

A long time ago in what seems like another lifetime I walked into a dojang to hear an instructor bark out, "You damn well better do it right every time. Quit wasting *my* time."

This was directed to a class filled with younger children, none older than 11 or 12, most closer to 8 years old. Their abilities were less than perfect, and this man, who is supposed to guide them along in their education of this martial art, claimed they were wasting "his" time.

I presume that the parents of every child under his instruction paid for the time spent in his classes; I certainly was not offered instruction for free. In fact, I was offered a contract that called for an exorbitant down payment and monthly fees that could have covered half my car payment. While that does not give the students the right to direct the direction instruction flows, nor the content, it does give them the right to expect to be treated fairly, and with respect. They are paying for that instructor's time; it is no longer his time; it's theirs.

Our students don't come to us with the expectations of satisfying the whims of our own egos; they come to us to learn. Some come because they want a black belt. Some come because they want to learn to defend themselves. Some aren't even sure why they come, but they do want to learn—and they can't be expected to perform on levels on expertise all the time. Kids will do pushups with their butts high in the air, sometimes they won't go down far enough; not all kids understand how to count off an exercise, not all kids know their left from their right (and neither do all adults.) Where a student falls short (of our expectations) and needs extra help, it does not cut into "our time." It is *their* time. They are the students, they are there to learn.

Our time comes later, and inflicting impatience on students is beyond counterproductive; it's mean.

* * *

I have never competed in a tournament; I enjoy watching sport karate and have indulged my curiosities a few times by attending tournaments as a spectator, but I choose to not compete and for that reason never bothered to learn the rules of point fighting, nor do I feel confident enough about the point system to stand as a judge for forms competition.

I do, however, understand fair play.

My partner has, in the past, competed and has been working with several students who are interested in tournament competition. All are relative beginners to the arts; one is a gold belt having trained less than six months, the others have trained less than a year but by virtue of rank are placed within the intermediate divisions. None care much about actually winning; they want the experience, they want to watch and to learn from other competitors, and all hope, I believe, to one day have the skills to compete at high levels.

I support that fully; just because I am not interested in competition does not mean I don't want to support my students who are; when they all registered for a small local tournament recently, I made sure I had the time off work and set aside other responsibilities so I could be there to watch and to cheer them on.

What I discovered was that the stereotypical Little League Parent has invaded sport karate with a vengeance. People crowded around the perimeters of the rings, screaming at their kids who were trying to get their way through forms, yelling "Come on! *Push!*" and other inanities. Children no older than 6 were the targets of parental angst; I felt for the ones who walked out of the ring having made some small mistake, knowing the verbal beating they were about to endure. It was worse during sparring, when parents would shout to their children "Hit him harder! Break his nose!"

What lessons are these kids learning? That winning the trophy means they're a better person? That not winning means they're scum? Or do they realize their parents look like jackasses in public, faces turning red and veins standing out as they scream as if their lives depended on it, all for the sake of a trophy.

I support my students' right and desire to compete, but I am appalled at the parental conduct I see during these tournaments. It's enough to make me very glad that the main focus of our dojang is not sport. It's enough, too, to make me wonder about the schools these kids train in, and what abuse to the ego do they suffer.

It's just a trophy.

* * *

"Ninety five percent of all fights go to the ground."

Where, I asked of the student spouting statistics, did that come from?

"I read it on the Internet."

The Gospel According To The Internet is rapidly becoming a pet peeve. While having expanded the resources for students to learn more about their arts, and giving voice to those who otherwise have no voice, it is also becoming the resource for misstatements, generalizations, and outright lies.

If, judging from the content of Internet sources, what one reads is always true, then the art which I teach has no self defense applications, martial arts don't work anyway, Royce Gracie is God, and 99.9% of all people who have ever tested for and received a black belt went to a McDojo, because, after all, they did not train in the "right art." I still haven't figured out what that "right art" is.

It's hard to make your students understand, when the fires of their curiosities are lit and the want to absorb knowledge like a sponge, that not everything they read is true, and not every black belt they meet online has actually trained. Some are book black belts, their knowledge deep and vast, but none of it comes from actual experience. Some are self-proclaimed black belts. Some are legitimate and know quite a bit, but are naturally biased towards their own art.

It would be helpful if, when a student first has a question, they would come to us. I value the Internet as a tremendous source for the wealth of information available and the bulletin boards and message centers where one can exchange ideas; I am rapidly becoming a skeptic and an eye-roller, though, when I hear the words "I read it on the Internet."

Just last week I read on the men's room wall that the blonde down the office corridor has potential date material and is cheap too boot...

Just because someone writes it, that doesn't make it automatically true. And just because it's on the Internet, that doesn't give it credibility.

Finding Joy In Things Tedious

My father recently pulled out a picture of me, sometime around the age of 8, sitting at the piano with a scowl on my face that suggested the first person to so much as blink at me would be a target for whatever ire could be raised by my pre-teen self. It was obvious that I did not want to be there, that being stuck at the piano was the last thing I wanted to be doing.

Getting me to practice, he tells me, was about as easy as counting dust motes on a windy day. I fought it all the time. I remember the irritation of daily practice and weekly lessons, and the frustration over being the only one of 3 siblings forced to endure musical Hades.

My father showed me the picture when he found me sitting at the piano, playing quietly and only for myself, for the love of the music and the comfort of being able to coax it from an instrument that in my youth had only yielded noise. He found it ironic that the same person who battled so hard to never touch a piano key again would find solace in the very thing he hated.

Perhaps it is ironic. As a child I could not have expressed any real reason I hated to play. It was one thing I could do

fairly well, something to which I was much better suited than
the pursuits I swore held more interest; I preferred to be outside playing baseball and football and basketball—even
though, in no uncertain terms, I sucked at them all. I wanted
to play ball and not piano because, I realize now, sports were
fun and piano was boring. Looking back, had I enjoyed the
music I was fumbling through, I might not have fought so
hard against the required lessons and half hour of daily practice. If I had been allowed to play the music I loved, instead
of Classics By Dead Guys, I suspect there would be no picture of my 8 year old self scowling in livid overtones, nothing to remind me that what I enjoy now, I detested then. Now
I get to choose my own songs. As an adult I never have to
plunk out a single note of Chopin or Mozart if I choose not
to.

Parents do what they feel best for their children. For
some of those children what their parents feel is best derives
not only from a feeling that directing the child into a particular activity is good on more than one level, but also because
parents tend to live vicariously through their kids. My mother
loved classical piano and had always wanted to play. I have
students whose parents always wanted to train, but for various reasons were never able to or allowed, so their children
train.

I don't agree, necessarily, with forcing a child into a
martial art. I have no problem with parents placing reluctant
students into classes with the notion that they should try it for
a time, and if they discover they truly hate it, then leaving is
an open option. Unwilling students can pose an ongoing problem for instructors and the students who honestly want to be
there—but there are always those few, and they have to be
contended with.

For the most part the reluctant students I have seen have personal issues with a fear of pain and a fear of fighting; martial arts may be their parents' choice, but not their own interest, and when you throw fear on top of the lack of interest, it's a recipe for a disinterested and difficult student. We all have them. We can't help but have them. We can, however, help them to keep an open mind, and to attempt to cultivate their own interest in the martial arts.

Our students don't have to play Chopin and Mozart every day—they don't have to stick to tried and true traditional teaching methods. Learning the basics and making them a part of yourself is long and tedious work, it involves repetition after repetition, and when you're 8 or 10 years old, and you don't want to be there in the first place, that repetition is more than work. It's mind numbingly boring, and a waste of time that could—in a child's mind—be better spent elsewhere.

Let them play their own music. Let them play. Children learn through play and through game-centered activity as well as they do through structure. There is no lack of discipline in play; on the contrary, games teach rules, and the benefits of following the rules, games can teach strategy and coordination. Games allow children to explore without the pressure of being the best, and allow them to learn through repetition that doesn't leave them more frustrated than educated. Martial arts oriented games can enforce the same basic fundamentals we would normally teach adults through structured class time, and do it in ways that have even reluctant students wanting to return, and to learn.

The games can be as simple as Simon Says; Simon says "front kick," Simon says "left punch, right punch, rear elbow," Simon says "front side kick, now do a back kick," nope buzz, I didn't say Simon Says.

You can play Mugger In The Middle, if you have enough foam body shields. Place one student in the middle of a circle or other students who hold foam shields. Each student with a shield is given a number; when you call out the number, they move in for the "attack;" the student in the middle then has to complete 1-4 techniques against the foam shield. The more advanced the students, the more advanced the techniques must be.

Set up obstacle courses for physical training and dexterity training. Start with having them run through a line using a grapevine side step, followed by a series of punches to a heavy bag, make a clean body roll over a line, then crabwalk through offset hand pads on the floor; if they make it that far, have another heavy bag hanging for a jump sidekick. The potential is limitless.

Don't be afraid of getting goofy. One of the most successful introductions to grappling that we've tried so far has been goofy enough to send the kids into spasms of laughter, but it works, and it helps build their upper body strength. We place two kids on the mats, in push up positions, and without letting any part of their bodies other than hands and feet touch the mat, they have to figure out how to leverage their opponent off center, how to grab their opponent's arm and pull them down without also falling themselves. We've also lined up 4 or 5 in a row in pushup position, and had them rotate in a circle, using only their hands and keeping their feet in place. They laugh, and they have fun, but it's *work* and it builds strength.

The tedious nature of learning through repetition doesn't have to be as agonizing as sitting there for hours on end playing music that has no interest to a child. It can be as simple as teaching through play on occasion, and it can help foster that desire to continue in the most reluctant of students, and some-day, with any luck, they can find their own comfort in the sheer joy of having taken the time to learn to do something, and do it well.

The Great Why'd Hope...
The Kids' Questions Answered

I have a female friend whose favorite question when given a new technique, or a theory, or just about anything else for that matter is "Why?" (et tu, Thump?) I suspect most of us wonder "why?" during class, or more like "why the &@$$?" are we doing this? Most students never ask. Either through shyness, assumption that questioning the instructor is out of line, or any other myriad of reasons, most students seem to accept what their instructors tell them at face value, and never question, even when they have doubts.

We have always encouraged our students to ask questions, even the sometimes annoying "why?", although it seems more adults than children feel free to probe, and surely the children have as many doubts as do the adults.

"It's simple," my nephew explained as if I were brain dead. "To the adults you're just another adult. To the kids you're a teacher. Teachers are supposed to give you the right information. Besides, no one wants to look stupid in front of everyone else."

And who could blame them?

We really did want to be able to answer the questions

that our younger students pondered over, without embarrassing them. During classes over a 2 week period we emphasized that point: we wanted to hear from them, and set out a locked box into which each student could deposit any question they so desired...especially "why?" Some questions were vague, some astonishingly to the point, and others...well, let's just say I really *don't* know that it's true Brittany Spears has implants, and I don't know why dodgeball is an integral part of gym class.

Why do we have to run, even during tests?

Mostly because I'm a sadist. But equally important is that running builds endurance, and endurance—along with skill—will get you through a tense situation. Plus, the more you run and the better you are at it, the easier it'll be to just run away if you need to. We make you run during tests because it tests *you*, your spirit, not just what you know about punching and kicking.

Why do we do class barefoot?

You learn balance better barefoot, and it's easier to learn to pivot correctly (which saves your knees from damage) without shoes on. Plus, your bare feet help me to see your foot positioning better, so I can help correct small mistakes before they become big mistakes.

Why do we have to wear jeans and t-shirts sometimes?

If you ever get into a fight, you won't be wearing your uniform. You'll be wearing street clothes, most likely. I like to hold class with all the students wearing their everyday clothes once a week so that you get a chance to practice your defense techniques with regular clothes and shoes on. Sometimes it makes a difference in how you move, and I want you all to be able to experience that before you ever have to find out on your own.

Why do I always have to stand in the front line? I like the back.

I like everyone to line up by height, with the tallest people in the back. If all the tall people stand up front and all the smaller people stand in the back, I can't see them very well when I'm in front of everyone. If I can't see you, I can't help you as well as I should.

Why can't I use the weight room?

When you turn 14, you can use everything but the free weights, and you can use those when you turn 16. We don't let anyone under 14 in there because until then, the strain of lifting a lot of weight over and over can damage your growing bones and your growth plates. Your health is the most important thing.

Why doesn't the pool have a diving board yet?

Because the pool is only 4 feet deep, and if you dove in you might break your neck.

Why are our uniforms white?

They're white because the white ones are the cheapest. You can wear any color uniform you want, though. You can even wear sweatpants and a t-shirt, I just ask that whatever you come to class in is clean and covers up everything that needs to be covered.

Why can't I get a black belt until I'm 12? Other places let kids get black belts at 6 or 7 years old and I don't want to wait until I'm old to get one.

I know other schools allow their kids to test for black belt when they are still very young, and I don't think there is anything wrong with it. Some schools use a poom belt, which is a junior black belt, and it's red and black; some just use a black belt. We thought about it for a long time before deciding to make our minimum age as 12; with few exceptions, most of the young kids we know who got their black belts before they were 10 or 12 quit, and within a short time forgot much of what they learned. They only stayed to get a black belt, not to really learn. We figured that if you really want to learn the martial art and not just get a black belt, you'll stick with it until you're 12, and you'll know that you really earned it. We won't test you for a black belt until you're 12, but when you turn 10, if you've been working hard, we'll let you test for the black and gold black belt candidate belt.

Why do you have to be 6 to take lessons? My brother wants to do it too but he's only 5 years old.

We decided that by the time most kids are 6 years old they would be able to pay attention better, and they wouldn't lose control of themselves outside of class and hurt somebody by playing around with their kicks and punches. Very young kids sometimes have a hard time controlling themselves, and they don't always understand that it hurts when they hit someone. By the time they are 6 years old, most kids understand, and most kids will follow the rules and not kick someone while they are playing.

Why are there so many mirrors?

Because I'm so vain…? No, we have lots of mirrors in the workout room so that you can see yourself and see how your body moves, and all the mirrors help me see you when my back is turned to you. That way I can still do what I'm doing, but still see if anyone needs me to stop and help, or correct small things.

Why can't we hit people in the face?

The bones in the face are fragile enough that a good kick to just under the eye or a hard punch to the nose could do some real damage. Since you're still growing, I don't want you to take that chance; we let the adults hit to the face, but only after they've made brown belt. By then they should have enough control to not hit hard enough to break someone's face. I know that the kids who are the same rank have the same (sometimes better) control, but it's not worth the risk. An adult can decide if they want to take that kind of chance.

Why can't we break boards? The older kids get to.

Give it some time. After you've trained for a few months more (about 5-6 months total) we'll introduce board breaking with kicks to you. We won't let you break boards with your hands until you are older, though, because punching a hard surface can damage the tiny little bones that your wrist is made of. Plus you have spaces between those bones, and the bones in your hand, called growth spaces. We don't want to damage those spaces, so your hands can keep growing normally. That is also why we won't let you do pushups on your knuckles. It's not worth the risk now, because it can affect you years later.

Why don't you ever go into tournaments, too?

Honestly, I like to watch tournaments, and if you or any other student wants to enter one, I'll be there to cheer you on, but I never trained in sport karate and I'd be out of my element there. Mr. Hunter knows much more about tournament play than I ever will, so he's the better one to teach you about point fighting and competition forms. I'm the better one to go watch and cheer loudly!

Why don't I have muscles like you and Mr. Hunter and Mr. Scott? I do pushups and everything just like you do.

Give it time. When you hit puberty in a few years your body will start making hormones, and if you keep working out as well as you do now, you'll start seeing bigger muscles then. If you keep exercising now, it will be a habit, and it good exercise has to be a habit to build big muscles and keep them.

Why does Mrs. Murphy smell better than you?

I think it's a girl thing.

Step By Step

My youngest son learned to roll over this summer. He surprised himself, and the sudden realization that he was not staring down at his toy on the floor but looking up at the ceiling made him cry. His brother laughed, his sister rubbed his tummy and told him he was all right. They proceeded to show him they could also roll, and spent the afternoon rolling around the living room, with a wide eyed infant staring at them like they were positively nuts.

My newest student learned to punch this summer. He surprised his parents, who were positive he would never look up from the floor, never think of striking out at anything, whether another person or inanimate object. His father puffed with pride, his mother cried. The boy himself uncurled himself, straightening his shoulders and standing tall, and punched again, with a room full of fellow students watching without knowing the effort this young boy made to simply look them in the eye.

My youngest son learned to lift himself up to his hands and knees, and to rock back and forth. He knows, on some level, that if he can figure out how to make those hands and legs move, he'll be able to get from where he's at to where he wants to be. If he can just get them to work in tandem, the world as he knows it will be his.

My newest student learned to say "no" and to walk away. He knows, deep down, that if he can walk away from a bully, not cave in to the fear, he'll be able to pull himself up from the darkness of being the class punching bag to the relative safety of being just like all the other kids. If he can just convince himself he is just as good and just as valuable as everyone else, the world will be his.

My youngest son learned to sit up, and to eat from a spoon. He knows the pure delight that the food that should be nourishing him feels just as good all over his face, squashed into his hair, and thrown at the dog, as it does in his mouth. Without knowing, he understands that the things we have to do don't have to be boring; he can take something as simple as eating or bathing and turn it into the most wondrous thing he has ever done. He marvels at the feel of rice cereal between his fingers. He squeals with joy when water is poured over his bare belly. The very basic things of life are sheer pleasure.

My newest student learned to jump, and to kick. He knows the satisfaction of a form done right, and that the simple gold belt form he has finally memorized the moves to is just as much fun for him as learning an advanced form is to a brown belt. No one has told him that he is working hard, that he sweats because the physical effort is as demanding as the mental effort. He smiles broadly when told he's doing well, he laughs when he falls because he knows he has another chance to do it right. He's having fun. The very basics of the art he's learning are sheer fun.

Those first few months of life are so filled with change and rapid learning it's easy to lose sight of the joy to be found in the very small things that are so important to learn before we can go on. Learning to roll, learning to rock back and forth on our hands and knees, smashing cereal into our hair and peeing in the bathtub are essential learning blocks; without them, sooner or later we'll meet something we can't figure out, can't get past. For the baby just going through those milestones, the process is nothing but fun, especially when the people around him giggle right along, aren't afraid to act silly, and don't rush the process.

The first few months of training are filled with as just as much rapid change and learning—and it's very easy, with so many students in need of our time and attention, to lose sight of the importance of those critical first steps, getting the foundation of each technique, and the joy it brings our students to not only learn them, but to be praised for the effort as well as the success. Teaching and learning in a martial art don't have to be deadly serious all the time; we enjoyed the learning process as infants, we can enjoy the learning process—as well as the teaching process—in our arts.

No matter what you've endeavored to do, it starts with those first small steps. If you skip them, sooner or later you'll trip. If we allow our infants to enjoy the process of growth, we wind up with happy, healthy children, and hopefully later on, well rounded adults. If we allow our students to enjoy the process of learning their art, we wind up with happy, well trained students, and hopefully later on, well rounded instructors. It all begins with that first little step, and the thousand to follow.

Separating The Martial From The Art

"There is art in what we do," is one of my partner's favorite expressions to make clear his reasons why we don't stick solely to self defense training. He uses it to defend the use of what some consider to be archaic forms, to defend the inclusion of music into training, and as reason to use as teaching tools things other instructors find unnecessary and a waste of time. With him you can argue until you are blue in the face that the martial arts were not created for dance, they were not meant as a socialization exercise; they were meant as warfare and for defensive purposes; he'll nod politely, and then tell you why you are wrong.

Most of what we teach is, in actuality, self defense training. The intention is for a student to walk in the door with that need, and to leave better prepared to face that possibility. It doesn't, however, take that long to teach someone to effectively defend himself if they are in good physical condition and have the ability to think clearly and react accordingly. The years that drag out between those first steps and being awarded an advanced rank are filled with much more than the teaching and learning of pure defensive structure. During all those small steps a student learns much about himself and his ability to deal with the world that surrounds him, and learns to control impulse. Hopefully at some point, he will also learn that the process is less involved with learning how to fight than it is with learning how to not fight.

A part of traditional martial arts training is the teaching of culture, passing on of familial traditions and histories; this separates the martial arts as a whole from the pure act of fighting. I trained in a Korean art, yet by deliberation I did not study Korean history or traditions; my familial roots are Irish. I was born in Ireland and raised as an American. I do not teach my students my Irish heritage, and I watch in amusement—and without offense—as some Irish customs are politely bastardized by jovial Americans. While we may train in an art form with it's foundations stemming from one culture, that does not obligate us to entrench ourselves in foreign traditions and ideologies; it merely affords us the opportunity to learn about those traditions if we so choose. To take on as ones own the trappings of another culture is, to some extent, to deny one's own heritage, something I am unwilling to do nor willing to inflict upon my students. That does not mean, however, that I would make unavailable the information they might choose to expose themselves to, nor does it mean I would strip away the art in my chosen style simply because it does have its foundations in another culture. It does mean that I recognize that part of the roots of my training, that it was never simply "just fighting" and it was a means for families to pass on their own traditions, martial and otherwise. As I will not participate in the (even unintentional) bastardization of my own culture, I will not risk doing the same to another.

It comes full circle to the notion that there *is* art in what we do, and to strip it of that in the name of "only teaching self defense" robs the style of the very base on which it was formed. Were a student interested in only learning to defend himself, there are less complicated and more direct ways to go about it. My primary goal is, always, to make sure that my students first and foremost learn defensive applications to the techniques they are taught, and that they understand how to combine those techniques effectively. Still, I take great pleasure in teaching them the art beyond the defense, I still take great pleasure in learning new forms myself and working to achieve a state of perfection I have not yet found.

I recently met a 6th degree black belt whose technique is impeccable; his form and execution are literally awe-inspiring, his knowledge of his art is deep and his ability to teach what he knows is natural. On the dojang floor he is fast and furious and spars as if his very life depends on it; however, in spite of the years of training and the mastery of his art, he might not fare as well in an all-out street fight as he does fighting in the dojang. Yes, he has mastered his art, he is a true master of his art, he is an able teacher and an apt student. Yes, his abilities *are* exceptional. His students are very fortunate to have him as an instructor. There are simply many out there with no formal training who could, weapon in hand, defeat him in an uncontrolled altercation. He admits this. His ego is not wrapped up tightly in his rank; he understands the difference between the fight in the dojang and the fight on the street. Because he understand this he is seeking, after a lifetime of training and teaching, additional instruction that separates the martial from the art and teaches the down and dirty of defending oneself in today's aggressive society.

Some might argue that this master is no master at all; if he does indeed believe that he could come out on the short end of a fight, then he has not yet mastered his art. Those same people might not believe that the founders of the arts they covet so deeply and tout so loudly as being the One True Art never faced a physical confrontation personally, yet therein lies some truth. One can understand deeply the principles of their art, have mastered the techniques and perfected each kata or poomse, and still know that they are not the epitome of a grandly staged martial arts movie scene; they know that no matter how many years and how dedicated they have been to their training that some young teenager hell bent on destruction could take them down before they could drop into a fighting stance.

On that same vein lies the raw, new student, who may not understand the fundamentals, has no concept of form or foundation, but who can instinctually come out the victor in an altercation. His instructor may be able to score on him easily and frequently in the dojang setting, may be able to upend him easily and have him on his back staring at ceiling tiles, but on the street, in a tempers-flared situation, that same student may have the advantage, and it does not make either person the lesser martial artist.

As the times change, as our cultures evolve—or dissolve—the needs of the individual for self protection change, yet our martial arts remain stubbornly set in the foundations of tradition. This is where the martial becomes the art, when the foundation needs to remain intact for the sake of continuity, and where practitioners should not be afraid of adapting old technique to suit new needs. It is worth doing the art for arts' sake, and worth passing on old techniques and methods of defense and attack; keeping those intact is as valuable to the style as is learning to reapply old technique to new defense.

It is a paradox; weeding out the old for the sake of the new while retaining the whole. If the art is to survive, the martial does need to be separated from the art, as well as kept firmly in place. It is the art in what we do.

Great Expectations

One thing I'm always curious about is why people gravitate towards the martial arts, why they seek out instruction, what makes them stay, and what pushes them to move on—either discontinuing their training altogether, or looking for another instructor. I don't think there's ever a wrong reason for beginning or ever a wrong reason for staying, but if someone is perfectly capable of defending themselves, I don't think it's always a bad idea for someone who has given it an honest try to walk away. I sometimes wonder, though, aside from the obvious desires to learn self defense or earning that black belt, and what it is they want from the school and the instructor they finally select.

What a student expects when they first start training and what they expect 4 or 5 years down the line are usually different things. That's normal; what keeps you training is often different than what spurred you to start in the first place. I first entered a dojang with a very selfish, somewhat skewed reason: I wanted a black belt. That's not what kept me there, however; over time my reasons for staying changed, and as I grew into those reasons, I also found a part of myself that didn't like some of the things I saw, and prodded me into leaving my instructor. I came to know what *I* expect from training and other people in the martial arts. I was curious about how other see things. Just what do people expect?

Finding out is simple: you just ask them.

With cooperation from other instructors in the area, I asked students to make out lists of their expectations; there were differences overall in what a beginner expected and what a long-time student expected, but there were several common things among all ranks and age groups. In no particular order:

That the instructor is competent and really does hold the black belt rank to which he lays claim. Even new students are now painfully aware that scattered throughout the martial arts communities exist a large number of McDojos and McDojangs. Just about everyone has a story about a friend or the friend of a friend who trained for a considerable amount of time under a less than scrupulous person who passed them self off as a black belt of varying degrees, only to discover later that this person left their own instructor after a year or two at the most. Others come to realize that their instructors have legitimate black belts, but lack the ability to teach well, or that they don't have the skills that most would expect of that rank.

Honesty. Students want the truth; if they lack in a particular area, they want to know. If they ask a question to which you have no answer, they would prefer to hear "I honestly don't know" to an answer that is laced with ambiguity, or worse "You're not ready for that." Students feel they have a right to honesty from their instructors.

That there will be no "secrets" when it comes to certain techniques. Most are no longer naive enough to believe that there are special, super-secret things to which only the cream of the crop will ever be privy; none of them want to be subjected to the subtle hints of secrecy, no matter what. When they are not ready to progress to the next level, being told that is usually enough. No one wants to be held hostage to their training by the notion that maybe, just maybe, there are some things held secret until they've been with their instructor for years.

That not only will basic technique be taught clearly, but how to apply them as well. Everyone learns the basics: front kick, round kick, side kick, punch, ridge hand, block, etc. Not everyone learns how to combine those basic techniques, or how to use them for defense. Students learn countless forms that contain all these techniques, but some are never told what those forms represent; they don't know that forward block is a reaction to an attack. They don't know the difference between an offensive sidekick and a defensive sidekick, because they are never taught how to apply the techniques they spend so much time learning. Students view this as a fundamental right of training; they want to not only learn each technique, but they want to know what it is used for, and how to vary a technique when needed.

That the instructor will support a student who chooses to explore other art forms after having a good foundation in the art in which they are currently training. No single martial art is "the" martial art; most students will have at least a basic curiosity about other martial arts and some will wish to actively seek out instruction in a second art. When a student has been training for a significant length of time and has grasped the basics to a degree of proficiency that assure the foundation they will bring with them is solid, there is no good reason to hold that student back. A few believe that they *must* have their instructor's permission before seeking out additional training; some know, without a doubt, that if they venture into other arts they will be banned from their schools. Most want that option, no matter what.

That the instructor and the students he or she uses as assistant instructors will demonstrate themselves to be good examples for their younger students. Students—no matter what the age—don't want to hear one thing from their instructor and observe the opposite. Parents want for their children instructors who not only promote good character and personal growth, but who live by their own words. It's the "Lead By Example" principle. Children notice the disparities as much as the adults do. They don't want to hear "never smoke, never drink" and then see a cigarette dangle from an instructor's lips, or see them with a can of beer in their hands. No one expects perfection, but everyone expects their instructor to be a good person. Being human is allowed, everyone makes mistakes, but by placing oneself up there as an example to his or her students, being a role model is a given. The children especially want to emulate their instructors; do you like the person you're showing to them?

That the instructor will not engage in "art bashing" not tolerate it from his students. The days of being able to convince a student that the art you teach is the ultimate martial art and that there is none better is long gone. Hearing you condemn any particular art only makes you look small to your students. They don't want to hear why Gimme-Yor-Do is a waste of time; they want to hear what *you* have to offer. When you can recognize the similarities and benefits of other art forms and are comfortable and confident enough to relate that information to your students, they recognize the truth.

That if the school's focus is primarily sport-oriented, it is not passed off as the best street defense. Also that if the school does absolutely no sport karate, the students who are interested in competition are told that right up front, and are encouraged to find someone who can teach them sport application. There are always those students who will want to compete, and there are always some students who want no part of the sport aspect of the martial arts and wish to learn pure defense. An instructor who has no experience in sport has the responsibility to be honest with his students; conversely, someone who has trained only in sport and has never made the connection between those techniques and defense application has the responsibility to let his students know that what he is teaching is sport. In either situation, students should be told where they can get what they need and what they want. It doesn't mean losing students; it only means giving them the option to expand their education.

Patience. No two students have identical levels of skill; some struggle deeply to learn very basic things. They require of their instructors an incredible amount of patience at times, and they are keenly aware of that fact. Even skilled students notice when their instructors lack the patience necessary to deal with others who seem stuck in one place; they want to see patience, as well as kindness and compassion.

That there will be classes available at reasonable times for students of all ranks, not just the best times for the black belt students; that students can expect individual attention to their rank groups when classes are comprised of a wide range of skill levels. Every student in a school has the right to expect a well rounded and fully balanced education in their martial art. It doesn't help the beginner to have all the classes available to him only taking place during the early afternoon hours when they would still be at work. It also doesn't help to have the advanced classes so limited in availability that progression is tightly limited. And in situations where the student base is small enough that all-rank classes are the norm, each group has a real need to have a good chunk of time devoted to their needs. Some beginners feel very self conscious trying to learn in front of a large group of advanced students, they need an incredible amount of attention dedicated to their skill level. In giving them that, many advanced students find that their progression is now limited because the bulk of time is necessarily spent on building those foundations for newer students. All require time; all require a balance.

Our students *do* have expectations other than our own. We're not mind readers—it helps to occasionally take stock of the people who have come to us with those expectations, and we need to find out for ourselves what they want, what they need, and what they really expect from us. We might even be surprised.

There's A Kind Of Hush All Over My World

My world is generally a pretty noisy place. Between all
the kids, my own and my nephews hanging off the rafters,
assorted family members and friends, noise is just something
I learned to live with and to love. All the toddler squealing
and infant crying, the teenagers arguing over the pool table
or the TV remote, all the general noises and clicks and hums
to the rhythm of life seem normal and important. Most important, all that noise distracts me from the sometimes loud
and insistent static that pounds my brain day and night.

My brain is a fairly loud place. Between work, the
dojang, my family, AADD, and surfing online, there's generally always something pinging around in there. Even at night,
when the house is quiet and the kids are asleep, my brain is
going at full tilt, trying to make sense of the things that get
shoved aside while I'm trying to deal with real life. I fight
with myself to keep from flitting from one thing to the next,
to concentrate and to pick through what needs to be dealt
with immediately. There's always something trying to push
its way into a thought—a friend, a child, a student. Perfectly

normal, I know most people deal with distraction. I deal with distraction that feeds upon itself.

Since I teach visualization to my students as a way to understand their forms and self defense drills, I thought it might be a good technique to use on myself: imagine the distractions as small fires, and put them out one by one. I started with what was essentially the biggest; I retired from my job. With government downsizing in the least likely places while expanding in the least necessary, I was offered the chance to retire early, and I grabbed it. It was like pouring a plane full of water on an out of control blaze. All the snaps and crackles and pops of that particular fire died out quickly, the noise abated, and it left me with a huge chunk of time to take stock of everything else that contributes to the static in my head.

Another slice of life that left a lot of static pounding between my temples has been my life online. Several years ago, before I married and had kids, I surfed into a chat room and found an affable group, people to kill empty hours with and who made me laugh, some that I came to consider as friends. Being private by nature, I withheld large pieces of myself, information that I wanted to share with no one— where I lived, what I did for a living. In the grand scheme of chat life, I didn't feel those things were important for anyone to know. No one needed those details in order to carry on a conversation.

With the growth of the internet, however, it's become almost impossible to hide behind a screen name; post a note to a newsgroup and anyone with even a little bit of savvy can trace the headers back to the originating ISP. I did years of backflips to keep that from happening, most times going so far as to dial up a carrier long distance and posting through anonymous email servers. Yes, I value my privacy that much. Where I live is no one's business. What I do to pay the bills is irrelevant. I never went online to engage anyone in a cyber-relationship, I made it clear that I was fully involved with someone and not interested in using chat rooms and email or newsgroups to find romance or even a cheap fling. I was clear on those points. I was not investing myself other than to spend some time talking to people I would otherwise never have the chance to meet.

Over time I did come to understand that some very good friendships could be fostered online. Old friends could be found, new friends could be made; two friends who found each other online married, and instead of being jaded and suspicious about their union, I was actually happy for them. They both deserve to be happy, and deserve to be happy with each other. Some friends demand more than others; some are not truly friends, but leeches on the soul, people who will lie to you, about you, wrap you around their hearts and then do everything possible to cut you from their soul in the worst ways possible. In the Online World, small things out of place loom large, and without bothering to get an explanation, some people will presume the worst of you and attack. When one such person caused me to question the woman to whom I had pledged my life, I should have been more wary, turned off the computer and walked away, but I didn't. When I realized that another had engaged in nothing but one lie after another, for no apparent reason other than to have things to talk about and to agonize over, I should have walked away, but I didn't. And when I realized that a third, someone who had poured out their soul to me, asked for advice, picked my brain about things that seemed important to their very survival as a Good Person, was yet another person weaving tales for the merit of good conversation, I learned.

I haven't ventured into a chat room since. The static that seared through my brain has quieted immensely.

After the years of trying to quiet the noises in my own head, giving credence to people who never really gave a damn in the first place, friends who were not friends, the demands of a job that intrigued me but took more of me than I had to give, I am tired. I am beyond tired; I have reached the point of sheer exhaustion. I cannot teach effectively, I cannot parent effectively, I cannot be the husband I need to be nor the man my wife deserves with the little echoes in my head and the fatigue that is left behind.

So, to that end, I am taking a break. I am turning the computer off, and I am walking away for a while. I will not venture into a chat room, nor a newsgroup, not even email. And so, to that end, I will not be contributing to *Martial Artists Wired* until my head has cleared and I am sure that venturing back online won't cause all the static to re-erupt. Murphy's World simply needs to stop spinning on its axis for a while; Murphy needs to recoup himself, eliminate the distractions, and concentrate on family and real friends.

I have enjoyed writing this column and have especially enjoyed the people I have met through email because of it. I hope to resume writing in a few months, when all the changes in my world feel natural and the quiet is more distracting than the noise.

So long, and see y'all later.